IN THE KEY
OF NIRA GHANI

In the
Key
of
NIRA GHANI

Natasha Deen

RP|TEENS
PHILADELPHIA

Running Press Teens
Hachette Book Group
1290 Avenue of the Americas, New York, NY 10104
www.runningpress.com/rpkids
@RP_Kids

Printed in the United States of America

First Edition: April 2019

Published by Running Press Teens, an imprint of Perseus Books, LLC,
a subsidiary of Hachette Book Group, Inc. The Running Press Teens
name and logo is a trademark of the Hachette Book Group.

The Hachette Speakers Bureau provides a wide range of authors
for speaking events. To find out more, go to www.hachettespeakersbureau.com
or call (866) 376-6591.

The publisher is not responsible for websites (or their content)
that are not owned by the publisher.

Print book cover and interior design by Frances J. Soo Ping Chow.
Jacket illustration by Frances J. Soo Ping Chow, Stock images © GettyImages

Library of Congress Control Number: 2018951805

ISBNs: 978-0-7624-6547-7 (hardcover), 978-0-7624-6548-4 (ebook)

LSC-C

10   9   8   7   6   5   4   3   2   1

For my grandmothers,

Kulsum Ally and Nazra Deen,

whose soft hands,

soft hearts,

and soft touch

taught me what true strength

looks like.

CHAPTER ONE

ISOLATION IS
AN ORGANIC COMPOUND

T he cow's eyeball floats in the formaldehyde. It's disembodied, a part cut off from the whole, just like me, but there's a difference between me and the cloudy orb. It stares out at the kids as though it knows the secret the rest of us are dying to find out.

McKenzie catches me looking at the jar. "Are you offended?"

"What?"

"We killed a cow. Are you mad at us or something? Aren't they sacred to your people or whatever?"

"I'm not Hindi," I tell her for what must be the millionth time.

"It's pronounced 'offended.'" She slows down the last word and says it louder, like I'm both illiterate and deaf. Smiles, then glowers when I don't smile back. "No one's trying to hurt your feelings. We just like burgers."

And right there is the reason that when I graduate high school, I'm taking off to a university that's light-years away from this town. And once I get to that faraway place, I'm disowning my parents for moving us to a neighborhood where I'm the only brown girl in the entire school and have to put up with idiots like McKenzie King. I go back to my staring contest with the eyeball.

"Why?" McKenzie chews on her gum, blows a blue bubble until it pops.

"Why what?"

"Why are cows sacred to your people?"

"They're not—" Crap. She has me on a technicality. I'm not Hindu, but some of my people are. I sigh. "My grandmother—who, unlike me, is Hindu—says the cow represents growth, life, and nonviolence. That's why it's sacred."

"But you're, like, Indian."

"No, I'm Guyanese." Judging from the look on her face, I've just fried her brain cell. Cell. Singular.

"Huh? But you're Indian."

"I'm from Guyana. So, yeah, I'm Guyanese Indian. West Indian. It's a different thing than—"

Her face lights up. "No kidding? Ghana? I didn't know you were African."

The next time my parents ask me why my science marks aren't higher, I'm going to tell them it's because of McKenzie. Because if

I were any smarter in physics, bio, or chemistry, I'd make a laser gun and vaporize the curly hair right off her pink scalp.

The bell rings, and I breathe out the tightness in my chest. For the next forty minutes, it's physics and the origin of the universe, and I'm craving every second of it. Physics has to have the answer because the other sciences are letting me down.

Biology says the visual system of humans is fine-tuned and able to detect minute variations in color and surface edges. So why don't the kids at school see me? Even McKenzie, who finds a way to get in my face every day, wouldn't notice if I disappeared. If the police came and questioned her about a missing brown girl, she'd say, "Brown? Like Indian? That reminds me, I want a burger."

The door opens, and the teacher comes in, but it's not Mr. Tamagotchi. It's a sub. "Sit down, everyone. Let's take attendance and get started." She flips through Mr. Tamagotchi's agenda and laughs. "Oh, an overview of string theory. I bet he's not talking about shoe strings or cheese strings."

No one laughs at her joke. For a second, I feel a rush of sympathy. This school is full of kids who've been together since pre-K. They're one collective brain, with acne and a BO problem. I've been at the school since my family moved to the neighborhood two years ago, and I'm still the one who's alone in class when the teacher asks us to pair up or make groups.

"Bye-bye Nira Gee-Hani?"

The class titters.

"It's pronounced Bee-Bee," I say, glad my dark skin hides the flush of pink creeping up my cheeks. "And it's Gah-nee. Bibi Nira Ghani. But I'm just Nira." I keep asking the school to use Nira instead of Bibi on the class lists. So far, my request is as invisible as I am.

"Okay, thanks." She moves to the next name on her list.

"Do you have any sisters, Bibi?" The question comes from one of McKenzie's buddies.

"No. Only child."

"Well, if you ever do," she says, "you should tell your parents to name them Cici and Didi."

McKenzie laughs. "They could go down the alphabet. Until they get to Zizi."

Her friend can't contain herself. "OMG. Can you imagine? Pee-Pee!"

"Double OMG, if it was Pee-Pee and a boy?"

In forty years, when I pick a senior citizen home for my parents—and I will because no way are those crazies living with me (and I don't care what Guyanese culture says about respecting your elders)—I'm picking the crappiest home out there. And when my parents ask why, I'm going to hand these moments out like bitter candy.

"Nira," says McKenzie, "we're just joking."

It's not an apology. It's what it always is, McKenzie being insensitive and justifying it by suggesting I don't know how to take a joke.

"Okay," the sub says when she's finished with attendance. "Give me a second to read over your teacher's notes."

"Hey, Nira," says McKenzie.

I hide my face behind my book.

"Nira, hey, Nira." She won't take the hint.

"What?"

"Did you ever ride elephants when you lived in Africa?"

I go back to reading.

"Sorry," says the teacher. "I may have missed a student. Who's Nira?"

Seriously. When I talk, does the air from my lungs lack the necessary force and pressure to reach people's ears? "Me."

She frowns. "Aren't you Bye-Bye?"

"I'm thinking of going bye-bye," I mutter, wishing someone near me would hear and get the joke and smile my way. But when I look up, McKenzie's gaze is on me, and there's no smile, just an unreadable expression on her face.

"Your teacher says I'm not to call on you if there's discussion or questions." Her frown deepens. "Why is that?"

"Because she always knows the answer," says McKenzie. "And he wants the rest of us to"—she takes a breath and mimics his nasal pitch—"'try and put in an effort. Come on, people, give Nira's vocal cords a rest.'"

McKenzie does a great impression. She even screws up her face the way Mr. Tamagotchi does when he thinks we're not trying to reach our potential.

"Oh, uh—" says the sub.

"It's not fair." McKenzie leans back. "Real life is all about collaborative problem-solving."

Unbelievable. Now she decides to grow a second brain cell.

"If she knows the answers, let her talk. Her people have been oppressed enough. She has a voice, right? Let her use it."

God, I hate my life.

———◇———

My usual table's waiting when I get to the cafeteria. At the back, in the corner. The other two walls are floor-to-ceiling windows, but only the popular kids get to sit in the sun.

Emily waits for me at the corner table. She's blond and blue-eyed with freckles, but she also has a scar from surgery on a cleft lip and thirty extra pounds from her love affair with chocolate bars. She waves when she sees me and points to the chair next to her.

I love her for that. I'm irritated with her for that. Waving and pointing. Like somehow the seats at that table are restricted access, instead of perpetually empty. I sit beside her but don't open my lunch bag. The smell of tuna wafts from it. I glance over at the popular tables, where they're eating pita pockets stuffed with deli meat, peppers, lettuce, and cheese. It looks so good; I can almost taste it.

McKenzie's there. Watching. She's always surveilling us. It's like she's part of the nerd police, the number-one detective of the uncool squad. I turn away so I don't have to see her and her perfect lunch.

I open my bag and peer inside. Remind myself I'm lucky to have food when there are probably starving children down the street. But the sandwich squishes in my mouth. Mom hasn't figured out the correct ratio of mayo to tuna. It's either dry enough to use as a desiccant or so wet, I think it could bring the fish back to life. I've tried to tell her I can make my lunch, but she's got this stupid hang-up about being a working mom. Like making my lunch makes up for not being there for parent-teacher meetings and assemblies, or baking me brownies after school.

Emily tips her cloth bag upside down, and four chocolate bars roll out. "It's been a multichocolate bar kind of morning."

"Four? What happened?"

"Rope climbing. This body's meant for a lot of things, but holding on to a piece of rope and climbing for the ceiling isn't one of them."

Oh, man. If she had to do it for gym, then so will I. Rope climbing. I barely have the upper body strength to throw off my bed covers.

"Did you see?"

There's the other reason Emily's at this table instead of with the pretty people. Her habit of talking in half sentences. It's like she's constantly looking for her psychic twin, the one who can finish her thoughts by reading her mind. "See what?"

"The band poster. They're doing auditions for jazz band."

The sudden image flashes through my brain. Me, under the pink and yellow lights, eyes closed, wailing a solo on a shiny trumpet. Reality raises the houselights. My parents will never let me try out. "Oh, cool."

"You should audition. You're amazing. Every time you play, I think of Neil Armstrong."

"You mean Louis Armstrong. He was the trumpet player. Neil was the astronaut."

"That's who I mean. You make me think of moonlight and defying gravity."

I may have only one friend in the world, but she's awesome enough to count for five. I tried to tell her that once, and she said, "Is that a joke about my weight?"

Which made me want to die until she laughed and said, "It's so easy to screw with you."

"You should try out." She shoves the purple paper at me.

It's a flyer advertising the auditions. Black musical notes border the edge, and in the middle are silhouettes of players holding guitars and saxes. My heart goes liquid at the thought of being one of those figures.

"You'd nail it like a hammer from the heavens."

I love playing trumpet, but I've never had formal training, never been tested by the Royal Conservatory. "It's a hobby." I get enough rejection in regular life. My ego's fine with that. But I'm sure it'll pack its bags and walk out if I set it up for extracurricular rejection by trying to compete with serious musicians.

"If I could play something, I'd try out." Her eyes go dreamy. The candy droops from her mouth and a line of caramel forms a soft U.

"You should still do it. Maybe there's room for a cymbal player or someone who can play a rain stick."

"I don't know. How will the audience see me if I'm hidden behind a rain stick?"

I don't understand why she's not at a table by the windows. She's funny and not in an ego-beating way. Emily likes her curves. She likes them so much, she doesn't mind laughing with them. With them, not at them.

My fingers find the tufts of hair growing on my jawline. I wish I liked my swarthy, dark face enough to joke about it. "Maybe we can drench you with hydrogen peroxide and luminol." My fingers fall away from my face. "You'd glow like a firework."

"We should do that for you, too. Then you can do an interpretive dance while I play." She mimes shaking a rain stick and starts laughing, and her face lights up with joy.

I catch everyone looking our way and realize we're too loud. Plus, Emily's miming could look like she's doing something a lot dirtier than shaking a stick. Before I can shush her or stop her movements, she elbows me and grunts. I follow the line of her gaze.

Noah.

When it comes to me and dealing with the rest of the kids, we're like positively charged magnets. We're the same, and you'd think that would bring us together. But magnets of the same charge repel each other. Not Noah. His differentness isn't a positively or negatively charged magnet. It's a gravitational pull, and it keeps everyone in his orbit.

I'm probably the only straight girl in school who doesn't lust after him. Not because I don't think he's attractive. He's all dark curly hair (please, can I touch it?), intense brown eyes (did you just look into my soul?), and great body (hold it against me). I'm just smart enough to know when someone's not just out of my league, but out of my universe, too.

"I heard he's trying out for jazz band."

Of course, he is.

"The guitar."

Of course, he is.

"But he might be adding sax, this time."

Shocker. Noah lives the life of legends and dreams. His dad not only gives him anything he wants, but he also takes Noah out of school for a week at a time. They go off and have adventures. Then Noah returns, carrying stories on his back, and wearing souvenirs on his arms and chest. Not the touristy kind. The other kind. The kind of shirts and accessories you get when you don't just immerse yourself in a culture, but you become the culture itself.

He's been gone for a few days. Today, he's wearing a graphic tee, worn jeans. The magical object in question is a leather band around his wrist. McKenzie and her crew are already rushing to him, touching the band, their fingers playing against his skin.

What is it about his different that makes it better than my different? Part of it is what he wears. Clothes talk. They have a conversation with people before you ever open your mouth. It's shorthand, but it's a layered, exotic language. They tell everyone about your hopes and dreams, how you see the world, and what you think of yourself. The kids at school, their clothes say they belong, that everything is theirs. My clothes don't say anything. They just apologize for my existence.

When the bell rings, I head to gym. It's my least favorite class, but I like the egalitarianism of the red sweats and white cotton shirts. If aliens landed and looked at us, no one could tell I'm poor. No one could see I don't belong. I finish dressing, lace my sneakers, and head into the gym. And I hold the fantasy of being connected as I walk through the doors. Clasp the daydream close until I'm forced to open my mouth and break the spell.

CHAPTER TWO

BAGGAGE COMES WITH REINFORCED HANDLES

alypso music booms at me as I enter the house, so loud no one can hear when I yell, "Hello? Who's home?" The smell of onion and garlic takes me into the kitchen where I find my mom and grandmother cooking dinner. Grandma's seated at the table, her arthritic fingers prying open pea shells. Mom stands in front of the stove, a worn apron tied tight around her nursing scrubs. Oil sizzles on the tawa while a plate of cooked roti sits beside her. Candles of differing colors and competing scents cast light and shadow on the counter, the stove, the table. The window's wide open, straining at its hinges. "What are we doing? Having a séance?" I blow out some of the candles.

"Nira! The smell—"

"Three candles aren't going to do anything with the smell of curry in the house. We have to talk." I shut off the music and sit next to Grandma. Since Mom's attention is on the stove, I slip my grandmother a chocolate bar. Milk chocolate, her favorite.

She gives me a warm smile as she slides it in the folds of her sari and goes back to shelling peas.

"Something happened at school?" Mom grasps the half-baked roti between her fingers and flips the dough to its uncooked side. "Is it your grades?"

"No." Not true. Something seismic happened at school. I decided to try out for jazz band. It happened when I was clinging to the rope, wishing I'd been gifted with upper body strength. Maybe it was the oxygen deprivation, maybe it was the humiliation of knowing everyone was staring and judging. Doesn't matter. What does matter is jazz band. I'm good with a trumpet. Great with it. The sound of a trumpet is the sound of my soul. Every time I play, it's like I'm communing with the molecules and atoms that make me, me. Maybe, if I play long enough, loud enough, good enough, my DNA will rearrange itself, and I'll figure out how to be smart, popular, and worthy.

Getting into band might be a way to get all that and more. The only downside is that I need Mom and Dad's permission. I have a better chance of scaling Mount Everest in a bikini and flip-flops.

"What happened at school?" She flips the roti in the air, catches and claps it, then throws it in the air again. Specks of flour and bread fly and settle on the counter. Her dark eyes hold my gaze. They see something is going on inside of me. "You need tea?"

Tea is my mom's answer to everything. The world could be invaded by zombies, and my mom would say, "You need tea?" And if those zombies cracked open my skull and ate half my brain, she would pat my hand and say, "Yes, tea with extra milk and sugar." Because dairy and sweetness solve life's problems. Then she would say, "I expect your marks to stay the same." Because that's my family's way. Whether you lose half your brain to a zombie or not, your grades must never suffer.

"I don't need tea."

She jerks her chin at the kettle and says to Grandma, "Put it to boil."

"Old woman, I don't need tea."

Grandma rises.

"I don't need—" Why am I fighting this? "Just a small cup."

"What happened?" Mom's concentration is back on the stove. "Wash your hands and help me."

Because you can't just talk in my house. You talk and work. "What am I supposed to do?"

Her brows pull together. "Find something."

There's a sink of dirty dishes. Over the rush of the water filling the sink, I watch the soap bubbles form a white castle. "I was wondering if maybe we could go shopping this weekend."

"You need something for school?"

"Kind of." I shut off the taps. The bubbles spill over the sides of the plates. I have to be subtle about this. My parents can see a frontal attack coming from miles away. I need a soft volley over their front lines. Clothes are the way to do it. If she says yes to the request, then I know she's in a good mood, and I can go for the Big Ask.

"I'd like a new pair of jeans. Maybe a shirt." As soon as it's out of my mouth, I regret it. Not because it wasn't a good idea. But because now that I've asked, I want them so badly, I can smell the new clothes, feel the smooth slip of the size sticker on the denim.

One outfit, but if I pair the jeans with other stuff, and wear the shirt underneath, it could take my bargain basement clothes to the main floor. Maybe. All I know is having at least one outfit that has the right graphic and brand name would be like having a magical shield. Maybe if I look more like the other kids, they'll pay attention. Imagine if I wore the outfit to the jazz audition. Me, a trumpet, and the right clothes? It would rearrange the stars and recombine my DNA.

"You don't need more clothes."

Mom's words rip me from my daydream. "Yes, I do."

"Your closet's full—"

"Of clearance shirts from stores that are so inconsequential, they don't even have a brand."

My mother shoots a dark smile at her mother-in-law.

"Inconsequential. And I thought your making her learn a word a day from the dictionary wouldn't pay off."

Grandma shrugs and keeps shelling the peas.

"You're making fun of me."

"You're making fun of yourself. You don't need clothes." She drops the roti on the plate and faces me. A thin film of sweat covers her forehead and chin. "And the money your father and I work for to buy your clothes isn't inconsequential, either."

"Why is it so bad to get a new outfit?"

Grandma rises and moves to the kettle as it boils.

"Why can't I have clothes that look like everyone else's?"

"Because it's a waste of money." Mom slaps a roll of dough on the counter. "Hundred-dollar jeans that you won't even want next year—"

"Yes, I will!"

"And what will they be worth the day after you buy them? Twenty dollars."

"I'm a good daughter." My face feels hotter than the stove, and I'm holding my breath so I don't scream. I haven't forgotten about the audition, and I can't risk getting her so mad she says no, but I can't let this go. "Do you know how many parents would kill to have a kid like me? They would love to get me stuff in return for my high marks, helping around the house—"

"Get them to buy you the jeans."

"I do chores—you think the rest of the kids in my class have to do chores?"

"We pay you an allowance."

"Big deal. The other kids get more money, and they do nothing!"

She turns back to the stove. "When they're forty, they'll still be living with their mother because they can't care for themselves."

I love how she says it without a hint of irony that Dad's mother lives here. Sure, it's my parents' house, but still, she's sharing a roof with her husband's mom. From the corner of my eye, I see Grandma dump two teaspoons of sugar in the cup. Her hand hovers over the sugar bowl.

"All I'm asking for is one outfit." The words are spoken through clenched teeth. My heart is beating so hard I hear it in my ears.

Grandma dumps another teaspoon of sugar in my cup and adds more milk.

"That costs as much as a dinner out. The conversation is over. That money is for your university. That's more important than jeans. We didn't bring you to Canada so you could put on makeup and tight jeans. You're here for the opportunities."

I want to barf. I'm so sick of hearing this lecture.

"Canada is safe—you think it's safe for you back in Guyana? You think the cops will protect you?"

"Stop." I put up my hand. "Stop before you tell me—again—how they're so corrupt you were able to buy your way out of speeding tickets."

"They're not all corrupt, but it's not safe like it is here. There aren't oppor—" Mom must see my eyes glazing over, because she stops mid-rant. "When you become a doctor, you can buy all the clothes you want. You can be a real star gyal."

Guyanese for a girl who's so good-looking, she can be an actress. My mother makes it sound like an insult. The fact I'm more likely to be cast as Quasimodo than Esmeralda adds a layer of sarcasm and cruelty to her barb.

"That's a million years away." My anger shoves the audition aside. I can be like my father sometimes. So caught up in the fight, I forget about the war. I feel his likeness, pounding around me, the shadow of him, warning me to shut up, but I can't.

Grandma looks my way; her dark eyes take in my face. Another teaspoon of sugar falls into my cup. If I don't have a brain aneurysm because of my mother, the tea is going to send me into a diabetic coma. On the bright side, either way, it'll get me out of school.

"What's a hundred dollars—and it wouldn't even be that much." It'll be more like ninety-eight, but still, that's under a hundred, right?

"Compound interest," says my mother.

"Huh?"

"Compound—What are they teaching you in school?"

Apparently not Negotiating with Stubborn Mothers 101.

"A hundred dollars invested over ten years, with ten-percent compound interest will get you two hundred dollars."

"For less than a hundred dollars invested today will get me . . ." I stop. I don't want to say "friends," because it'll look like I'm trying to buy friends with clothes. Which I'm kind of doing. Which makes me wonder why I want to hang out with kids who care more about brand names than my heart.

Oh yeah. Because I don't want to spend my life alone and I want others to see me and Emily for the kind of cool people we are. If it takes a pair of hundred-dollar jeans or a graphic on a shirt, so be it.

"If the kids can't like you for who you are, then they're not worth it. Clothes don't make the person."

If she starts talking about what's on the inside that—

"It's what's on the inside that counts."

Grandma hands me the tea and shuffles back to the table. She sits with a grunt and resumes the shelling of the peas.

I set down the mug. "Really? It's what's on the inside that matters more?"

Mom sighs.

Grandma shakes her head, stands, and moves my way.

"Then why don't you wear your pajamas to work?" I ask.

Mom stares at me.

"If clothes don't matter, then why don't you go in jogging pants?"

Grandma hip checks me to the side, flips on the tap, and refills the kettle.

"That's not the same thing. Of course, clothes matter—!"

"Exactly!"

Her breath hisses through her teeth. "You have to wear clothes. You don't have to wear expensive clothes."

"If I want to fit in, I do. I'm the only brown girl in the school."

"And you think wearing cool jeans will suddenly make you blend in?" Sarcasm laces her question. "You think they'll walk in and say, 'Oh my god! Nira turned white!'"

"No, but it would make me stand out less." I take the tea. "When we left Guyana, you gave me this big speech about the cosmos. Said how the sky was filled with more than just stars. It was filled with planets and meteors and comets. And I'd never learn about all those things if we stayed in Guyana and played with stars. Well, guess what, Mom. Saturn and Neptune don't like to play with you if you look like a meteorite instead of like one of the planets."

"You look like one of the planets to me. In fact, your head looks like it's up Uran—"

"Juvenile. I should've guessed." I continue my dramatic exit.

"So that's it?" She calls after me. "You're not going to wash the dishes?"

"You said talk and do something." I make eye contact. "I'm all talked out, and you got the last word. Just like always."

Her lips press together. In the background, the ghee sizzles on the tawa.

I leave the kitchen as Grandma ladles another teaspoon of sugar into a mug.

I sit on the bed, playing my trumpet. Technically, it's a B-flat pocket trumpet. It has all the range of a regular instrument, but it's smaller. In other words, "real" musicians don't use it, except for practice sessions. Then again, "real" musicians didn't learn how to play from watching online videos.

Still, it's a trumpet. I know how to turn its valves and keys into music, and it feels good in my hands. Cold and metal. As long as its weight is on my palms, the world still makes sense.

I wish I lived in a world of music and not one of academics. Music makes sense to me. Notes are broken into whole, quarter, half. They always count for the same time, no matter what. Low notes take the bass side, higher ones get the treble. If I play one note and then another, it always makes the same sounds. A melody is always a melody.

The only thing in my world that's remotely the same is math, but math doesn't move me like music. I put the mouthpiece to my lips and blow a middle C. The sound is clear and pure. From there, I run the scale, then my fingers find their life, my ears wake to the sound, and not-so-suddenly, I'm playing "Georgia on My Mind." I hear the voice of Ray Charles in my head, crooning his love for Georgia. Telling her that she fills his thoughts and gives him peace. It's my love song to my trumpet. He's my Georgia, and he's secure enough in our love that he doesn't mind me calling him by a girl's name.

Forty-five minutes later, Mom finds me in my cramped room. She knocks but doesn't wait for me to say anything before she comes inside.

I sit up and prepare for round two.

"Let's go. Your father is home."

For a second, hope lifts me to the sky. Is Mom taking me shopping? The chance to ask her about the band audition surges in my heart, so powerful it makes my chest ache, and my temples hurt. "Go where?"

But she doesn't say "the mall." She says, "Your cousin's."

I groan and flop back on the bed. Last year, my dad's brother moved to town, complete with his perfect wife and perfect child. When we left Guyana, the government kept our money. It was a tactic to keep citizens from emigrating.

But thanks to an election and a new political party in power, my uncle was allowed to keep his wealth. So instead of a too-small bungalow in an okay part of town, his family lives in a two story with a walkout basement, in the newest neighborhood.

"We're leaving in five minutes, Nira. Brush your hair."

Brush your hair, I mime the words at her back, then slam my mouth closed when she whirls to face me.

"I don't like how you're talking to me."

Me neither. It's not in my genetic code to talk back to adults or question my parents, but this life makes me feel like I'm a medieval prisoner, tied to four different horses. Myself. School. This country. My family. And everything is pulling me in a different direction. I don't understand why there can't be a compromise. Why everything I want has to be a losing battle. "I'm sorry," I tell her because that's genetic to every kid. We always have to be the ones who're sorry.

She sighs and sits on my bed. "I know this isn't easy." She reaches into her apron and pulls out a twenty-dollar bill. "Here. I was young once."

"What's this?"

"For your jeans. Put it with your allowance money. We can go this weekend to the mall."

The money suddenly feels hot as fire in my hand. I've won the battle, but the way my mother says it burns me. Like the cost of my win has been a small part of her soul.

"Take it back," I tell her. "I don't want it."

"Nira!" The force of her turn makes the mattress bounce. "You come home, and you can't even say, 'Hello, Mom. How are you, Grandma? Thank you for making dinner. Thank you for putting a roof over our head.' No, you come in and start yelling about how you need clothes and what terrible parents we are for bringing you here. Now you tell me you don't want the money?" She storms for the door. "Your eyes pass me, girl."

Your eyes pass me. Guyanese for disrespect of the highest order. The accusation stings. She's the one who's being disrespectful. I didn't want the money because it made me feel guilty. Now she's making it like I'm a bad person for wanting to fit in. Like something's lacking in me. She slams the door closed, and I'm not sorry anymore. I don't care if giving me money cost a bit of her soul. She's got loads to spare.

I pull the brush through my hair so hard it makes my scalp sting, then I wrench my hair into a ponytail. I'm going to be ready and waiting in the car. She'll see, I'm a good kid, and then she'll feel bad. I don't deserve her yelling at me.

I'm so locked in the internal battle, so lost in the imaginary fight I'm having with her, I almost run into Grandma when I swing open the door.

As placid as a quiet stream, she moves past me to the bed. "Come. Sit." She glances at the floor and picks up a crumpled piece of purple paper. The jazz auditions. It must have fallen out of my pocket. She unfolds it, smooths the creases, then places it on my nightstand.

I sit beside her. "Thank you for the tea."

She smiles and takes my hand, and I feel the squares of chocolate in her palm. "For you."

"No, I buy the chocolate for you—" I pull away to inspect them. The packaging on the chocolate makes me pause. "This is Ghirardelli. I bought you them months ago. Aren't you eating?"

"I eat and share them as I choose."

A stab of jealousy goes through me because I know who gets to share with her. Farah.

She holds my hand, again. Her fingers are a world of their own. Soft and strong. Calloused and arthritic. I twine my fingers in hers and feel the breath between us.

"It's not easy to be the only one who doesn't fit in when everyone else has a place."

I think of Emily and feel a pang of guilt. "It's not just me who doesn't fit. . . . It's just, I'm the most different. And I got this idiot girl who keeps thinking I'm Hindi."

She laughs. "If she asks hard questions, I'll answer for you. Here." She presses money into my hand.

I look at it and feel sick. Twenty dollars. That's a hundred for her. "No, Grandma."

"I'm not so old I don't remember what it is to want a cute dress."

"Yeah, but Mom gave me twenty and if you give me twenty—" I trail off and wait for her to understand.

"What?" she says. "You can't do the math? It's forty." She sucks her teeth, a sure sign of her irritation. "And they think Guyana is backwater." She shifts her weight, drives her hand into my thigh as she heaves herself up. "What are they teaching you in this country?"

"Obviously not as much as you can teach me."

She looks back, smiles over her shoulder. Worry wipes it from her mouth. "Nira, you can want all the clothes and friends and romance you want, but those aren't the things that matter. If you can read and write, that's what matters. The rest of it is garbage to distract you."

"I know, Grandma." Education. The theme song of our family and it's on infinite repeat on our playlist.

"Brush your hair and get in the car. There's a bag of roti by the door, bring it."

"I did brush my hair!"

"Do it again. You look like you've been electrocuted."

"That's the humidity." I follow her out the door, arguing with her and trying to explain moisture and hair, and my need for hair products that Mom won't buy, and loving my grandma for getting me even if she doesn't understand me.

CHAPTER THREE

ENVY IS THE NEW BLACK

The four of us form a crescent moon around the glass double doors of my cousin's home. Aunty Gul answers it. She doesn't open both doors, but cracks one open and allows just enough space for us to see half of her. Like she can't see through the giant windows in the doors and know we're not strangers. Like she can't tell it's family and not marauders ringing her bell. Like marauders would ring a bell.

She's dressed in slacks and silk and pearls. "Come in, come in! It's so cold out there! Hurry, all the hot air's escaping!"

We're forced to shuffle into the house one at a time, because she won't open the door all the way. Mom, with her generous curves, looks like a too-stuffed sausage trying to fit into its casing. I squeeze in the gap after Grandma. Dad waits until last. Then it's empty hugs and air kisses and Aunt Gul's spicy, cloying perfume.

"Nira, don't you look beautiful." She casts a critical glance at my hair and touches my shirt with a meaningful cluck. "Such an unusual outfit."

I tuck the hair behind my ears and turn from her gaze. She hugs my mother as I take off my shoes and line them up with the others along the wall. I'd been hoping for a night of just family, but judging from all the shoes, Aunty Gul's decided to throw a party. Which must mean they've bought something new and want to unveil it.

"Safiya, so happy to have you here," she says, and embraces my mother.

"I brought curry and roti."

"Yes," says my aunt with a laugh. "I can smell it on your clothes. Next time, you should light candles."

My mother shoots me a look sharp enough to cut concrete.

"Of course, your house is too small to do what I do," continues Aunty Gul, "but I put a camp stove in the garage. That's where I cook all the smelly food." She pivots to Grandma. The hug they give each other is a bare meeting of hands on shoulders. "What a—distinctive—outfit." She eyes Grandma's blouse with neon-colored parrots and her dark-wash jeans.

"It's happy, and the colors remind me of home." She moves to Farah. They hold each other as though it's been months instead of seven days. Grams spends two weekends a month with Farah and the rest of the time at our house. I shouldn't be jealous, but I don't like how they hold each other and whisper, and I don't like how Grandma slips her the chocolate. It sucks to be petty, but Farah has everything. I wish Grams would look my way and roll her eyes, but when she meets my gaze, she smiles, then goes back to whispering with Farah.

Aunty Gul threads her arm through my mom's and leads her down the hallway, the heels of her shoes clicking on the hardwood. "Nira, Farah's friends are downstairs."

Oh, hold me back. The Farahbots. I should check my pulse and make sure it hasn't flatlined with all my excitement. I wonder if I could fake a twisted ankle and avoid having to go downstairs. Better yet, I wonder if I could fake a coma and get out of this life. I shuffle to the curved staircase that sweeps into the basement, but just then, the flurry of footsteps sounds from below. They race up the stairs.

My first thought is, they're so Indian. Nose rings, bracelets, kohl-rimmed eyes. Then I wonder what it must be like to be at their school, to walk down the hallways and see other kids that look like them, to be part of a culture that everyone understands. They head to their families, perfect Indian dolls with the right clothes and hair, full of confidence that this world and its privileges are theirs.

It's not Mom and Dad's fault that we moved into a neighborhood with a school full of European kids and hardly anyone of color, but it's another reason to resent Farah. Thanks to her parents' money and entry to a private school, she gets to be surrounded by people who look like a reflection of her. If I wanted to attend a similar school, it would add three hours of bus time. Mom and Dad shut me down the first time I asked for the transfer.

"Nira." Like her mother did with my mother, Farah threads her arm through mine and hauls me toward the kitchen. She presses her face into my neck. "Smells like your mom made curry. Goat or chicken?"

My teeth clench. Like mother, like daughter. "Chicken." I twist out of her grasp and away from the sweet scent of her perfume.

That's the full conversation because then we're in the spacious kitchen and grappling for a spot among the arms and elbows of everyone else. The food's laid out on the counter. While everyone's reaching for plastic plates and utensils—"The recycle bag is by the back door!" yells Uncle Raj—I stare at the food. Pumpkin beef and rice, garlic pork, pholourie, and chana. But it's not only Guyanese food. There's southern fried chicken, pot roast, baked macaroni, and french fries. I have to bend close to catch the scent of cumin and cinnamon, to inhale the onions and butter.

It's as if even the food is too scared of Aunty Gul to smell like itself in this house. I wonder how it is that so many cultures can coexist on a table but not in real life. Then I remember, the food is dead. It takes a while, but everyone fills their plates. They balance with care as they tiptoe to their chairs in the spacious dining room, careful not to spill sauce on the floor.

"Nira, you lead us in prayer," says Uncle Raj, when we're seated.

"Uh, which one?" At the table are Christians, Hindus, Muslims, a couple of agnostics, and atheists.

"Any," he says with a smile.

I bow my head and close my eyes. *"Allahumma barik lana—"*

One of Farah's friends bursts out laughing. "Oh my god, you sound so white when you say it!"

The heat of my blush blisters my skin, but I keep going and ignore the giggles of the girl. I keep my eyes closed because I know Farah's laughing, too, and I don't need to see it. Conversation starts. I stuff myself full of chana and callaloo. Then I hear it. Aunty Gul.

"The weather's getting cold, Nira." She smiles as though trying to show all her teeth. "Think this'll be the winter for you?"

"Gul—" My mother shoots me a glance and raises her hand.

But my aunt is on one of her favorite topics. Embarrassing me. "When she was little," she tells the crowded table, "and came here, she was so struck by all the white people, she thought she would turn white, too."

The adults cast me indulgent smiles.

Farah's friends look at me like I'm a freak.

"Every winter." Aunty Gul laughs. "She called them the sky people because the first time she saw a white person it was on the plane. Blond hair, blue eyes. Freckles. Remember, Nira? You thought she made the plane fly." Another shrill laugh.

"I love Nira's imagination," says my mother. "A doctor needs creativity to heal people and create medicine."

Trust my mother to defend me while still pushing me to become a doctor. Still, I appreciate her efforts. If it were only adults here, I'd cheer her on and make her tea when we get home. But Farah's there. Staring at me. Her friends are looking everywhere but me.

"And the clothes!" Aunty Gul claps her hands. "She thought it was the clothes the stewardess wore that made everyone listen to her. For months, she drove her parents crazy because she wanted the same outfit."

"I was only five, and thinking I was going to become white made sense. It's different now"—I glance at the Farahbots—"there are tons of colored people, but when we got here, the town had no brown folk."

A flash of pain speeds across my mother's face and I'm filled with guilt. I had been so proud of my parents for starting this adventure, so excited to be a pioneer. I'm still proud of them, of her—even if I'm mad at her at the same time—and I can't stay silent while Aunty Gul aka Donkey Voice honks and brays at my mom. "Yes, Aunty Gul, it is getting cold, but winter's not coming for a while."

She frowns then remembers she started the conversation by talking about the weather.

"When it does, we should all take a drive to the mountains and see what we can find. If you're up for it." I smile at her. "It takes a certain kind of personality to step into the cold and the untracked snow and make their own path. It doesn't take any kind of bravery to follow in footsteps that are already there."

Aunty Gul's face tightens.

"The food is delicious. I'm so glad you guys moved here to join us. It's nice to be with family."

My dad clears his throat, but I catch the twinkle in his eye before he looks away. Mom hides her smile behind a mouthful of cook-up rice.

The conversation, thank god, goes off me and turns to the economy. I'm happy to ignore them and eat my curry and roti. After dinner, I flee from the table.

"So, Nira, let's gaff a little." Uncle Raj blocks my exit.

No, no, no. The last thing I want to do is talk to him. "Uh, I was going to find Grandma—"

"Come, come, let's lime."

Great. From a conversation to a full-on let's hang out. I nod before he invites me to live with them.

"How is school treating you?" Uncle Raj puts an arm around my shoulder. His other hand holds a glass of Guyanese rum. That's stuff so strong if he belches he'll set the curtains on fire.

"Good."

"Your marks?"

"Mostly As."

"Mostly?"

"A couple of A minuses."

"You do the best with what God gave you, right?" He claps me on the back. "Farah's all As."

What a shock.

He takes a sip of his drink. "And the university science contest?"

I hate him for purposely being vague. Pretending he doesn't care enough to remember the full details of the competition. "I came in second."

"Farah came in first."

I know. He knows I know. "Wow? Really? Congratulations."

He waves his hand. "These science contests. Now we must arrange for her to go to NASA for some visit she's won. I'll have to take time off, and she will miss school. For what? To visit some pool where astronauts swim."

It's taking everything I have not to yell and scream. He's bragging by pretending he doesn't care. I wish they'd never left Guyana.

Farah bumps me on the shoulder. "Let's go to my room."

"I was telling her about how you won that contest." He makes a face. "The expense of having to stay at a five-star hotel." His gaze shifts my way. "My back. I need a special kind of mattress."

I think I need a special kind of pillow. The kind that would smother him.

"Why all the people tonight?" I ask as I follow Farah. My foot touches the deep carpeting of the steps. "Your mom only has company when . . ."

She shrugs. "New car and the bar-be-que."

"Didn't you just buy one? The car, I mean."

"Newer car."

"Oh. Nice. What kind?"

Another shrug. "It drives itself."

We have a rickety minivan that doesn't even have air-conditioning. Dad refuses to buy a new—or newer—car because this one's so old, he can fix it if anything goes wrong. "These new models," he says, "They're more computer than machine. Where's the fun in that?"

When I point out the fun in not melting into the seat during a hot summer day, he just makes a face and dismisses me with a wave. "This one is better. I can take care of it, and it takes care of us." Which all translates to money. We don't have money to buy a new vehicle, and Dad lying about the convenience of tuning up is better than him admitting we're poor.

I follow Farah and wonder what it must be like to have so many things that one more thing doesn't matter. In the background, I hear my dad talking, waxing poetic on his view of child-rearing. Academics, strict curfew, chores, with the occasional sleepover or playdate. "Give them too much time," he says, "and they'll get lazy. An idle mind is the devil's workshop. If you let Nira on her own, all she'll do is watch TV. She'd end up in a gutter."

That's my dad's worst-case scenario for everything, ending up in a gutter. Don't study and you'll end up in a gutter. Stay away from drugs, or you'll end up in a gutter. Eat the broccoli, or you'll end up in a gutter. Like broccoli has that kind of power. As if. Everyone knows that's brussels sprouts.

One day, I want to meet these mythical, lazy children—the ones that end up in the gutter. None of my memories of Guyana include dirty kids clogging the drain pipes and sewers.

I sigh and follow Farah. The Farahbots try to follow, but she stops them with a glare. Oh, the joy—it's just Farah and me. Quick, someone catch me before I faint from the thrill of it all. The girls move back to the living room, where their parents sit, and I follow my cousin.

We get to her bedroom, aka my fantasy room, and I keep my face devoid of the envy I feel. She's painted it in orange and hot pink—too warm for my taste, but it's big, bright, and decorated with black and whites of Marilyn Monroe and Audrey Hepburn. Farah deposits herself by the window seat and cranks open the bay window. "Want one?" She holds out a cigarette.

"Uh, no, thanks."

She gives me the kind of smile an adult gives a kid. "You're so good." And she makes "good" sounds like a cuss.

"Not really. I just don't want to die a slow, lingering death."

"Like I said, good." She lights the cigarette and takes a drag.

I sit on her bed and sink into the pile of goose down duvet. "Congratulations on winning the competition."

"Like there was any doubt. Of course, I'd get first." The ash of the cigarette is flicked through the open window and disappears into the night.

That's what I love about Farah. Her modesty.

"We got four tickets. Do you want to come? We'd pay for everything."

My vision of hell. Stuck in a room with the three of them and being reminded at every moment they're paying for me. "I'm not sure. There's school and stuff. And tryouts for jazz band." The last part slips out, and I immediately regret my words.

"Your parents are letting you try out?"

I shrug, feeling superior at the reluctant note of longing in her voice. "Not sure if I'll try out. I might." The only thing Farah doesn't do is play an instrument. Her parents, like mine, think it's a waste of time. Sports and academics. That's her life. I can't resist the temptation to shove it in her face, that there's one thing I can do that she can't. That my parents, unlike hers, might let me break out of the Guyanese mold our parents seem determined to bake us in.

"You still use that toy trumpet?"

Any pride and smug self-satisfaction I have disappears. I say nothing because my emotion will betray itself in my words.

Farah squints, and her gaze travels up and down me. "Yeah, I guess it's a bad idea to have you come. Five stars and all."

While the liquid warmth of embarrassment pours through me, she takes a final drag, grounds the cigarette on the shingle. "Come on. Mom made salara for dessert."

I pass by the living room on my way to the kitchen. Grams stands and heads to the stairs, to Farah. After I help myself to some dessert and tea, I hide in the library. When we drive home three hours later, my parents' conversation isn't about the car but the BBQ.

"Too many things," says Mom. "Stove, broiler. It even plays music. Why do you need all that stuff? A pit with charcoal. That's it."

"The rotisserie." Dad stares ahead. "That would be good. Sit outside and watch it turn."

That's my parents' philosophy with everything. Mom will settle for whatever she can get, and Dad would rather sit and watch than participate. It hits me, not for the first time, how different I am from them. How they'll never understand me. I turn my face to the window, watching the streets pass by and wishing I could get out and walk.

———————◇———————

When the weekend comes, I'm happy to escape the house. Mom wants to go to the mall. She's determined I get clothes now, but I know she'll never set foot in the stores I want. I brush her off by telling her there's a sale in two weeks. The chance to save twenty percent on clothes is enough to quiet her.

I check in with Grandma as she comes in from her ritual walk. "How's the weather?"

"Take some mittens." She gives me a kiss, and I leave.

I head downtown, to the sketchier but cooler side of town. It's a miracle my mental parentals allow me this freedom, but it was a scheme executed after weeks of planning. I told them Steven Spielberg comes up with ideas for his movies when he's driving. It could've been walking. I wasn't clear on the activity. My push was that mundane activities encourage brain processing and problem-solving. Then I dangled the rumor that Sally Ride—a scientist!—solved stuff while having baths and naps.

My parents heard what I wanted—doing trivial stuff is good. I won the right to take bus rides. They don't know I get off the bus and walk around. As long as I don't get mugged, I'll be fine. If I'm murdered, that'll work in my favor because then Mom and Dad won't be able to kill me for disobeying them.

The bus holds a spattering of sleepy shift workers and a couple of university students. They rock back and forth to the bus's rhythm. We're lost in our private worlds. Any awareness of each other is peripheral. I follow the tracks the rain makes on the window and count the landmarks until my stop.

La Pâtisserie bakery is my signal to get off. On my way back, I'll stop in and get Grandma a chocolate croissant. I climb down and enter a neighborhood of mom-and-pop shops—businesses that have been there since the pioneers rode their wagons in. I walk to the instrument shop, built back when the neighborhood was full of jazz musicians and blues singers. Now the neighborhood's in the midst of falling apart and resurrecting via gentrification. The mom-and-pop stores are losing to box chains. But the instrument store, Reynolds, remains. It's worth the hop over a used condom and the scent of urine from the doorway.

The bell tinkles as I step inside, away from the cold rain and gray sky. The shop is warm, and the faint scent of wax adds lemon to the air. Guitars line the walls. Old-school acoustic for the sensitive types, lipstick red for the rockers. What I want is in the back.

Alec, the cashier, looks up from his phone and gives me a nod. "Nira. Haven't seen you in a couple of weeks. Already buried with back-to-school stuff?"

"I was studying for a science competition."

"How did it go?"

I shrug, and he smiles. "Placed in the top five but you're pissed that you didn't get first."

"Next time I'll try harder."

"You should put that on a T-shirt."

"Don't need to," I tell him. "It's tattooed on my skin."

His eyebrows go up. A smile curves his lips, and he gives me a quick once-over. "Yeah? Where?"

"All over. It covers me in a blanket of brown."

He laughs and slides off his stool. "Here to drool?"

"Think of a better way to start the morning?"

I head to the back. He trails after me. The wall is wood and hanging on every available space are rows of trumpets. They gleam in silver and gold under the lights, their metal burnished. My longing is reflected in their bells.

"Some guy brought in a Bach Stradivarius."

I close my eyes. Imagine the feel of the metal along my fingers, the sweet pain of my lips tightening to hit the high notes, my burning breath as I try to make the music last as long as I can.

"You wanna see it?"

God, yes. We sneak in the back.

"If the boss comes, we're looking for help, and you're interviewing. That's your cover."

"Are you really looking for help?"

"Yeah." His eyebrows go up. "What do you know about music?"

"I know what I like."

He laughs.

This job would be my calling. Spending a day surrounded by these walls and having someone pay me for it. Maybe my folks would visit me at work. They would see how happy I am and unchain me from their burdensome need for me to become a doctor. "What do I need to know?"

"Not much. If you know a bit of everything with instruments, that's cool."

Jeez. He may as well have asked me to redesign the Large Hadron Collider to run on cream cheese. This store has everything—guitars, pianos, tubas, violins. I'd have to know the difference between an acoustic and Spanish guitar. Plus, all the tiny things, like strings and picks, and how to troubleshoot sticky valves.

It's not like I can't study for it. I'm brown, and I'm an immigrant kid. Studying is in my DNA. But trying to wedge the knowledge in between studying for my regular academic challenge classes is a feat for Hercules. "Can you train?"

The downward pull of his mouth says it all. "If it were up to me, I'd say yes. But Masao is all about his people being experts. Customer service and whatever."

"Too bad." The words are light, but my heart is heavy. Why did

I even ask? The heavens would have to crash down, and the voice of God sound before my parents let me have an after-school job.

That's the problem with being in this country. I see all the things I could be and do. Everyone and everything, from TV to school and books, encourages me to shoot for the moon. But I'm a poor kid who wasn't even born here, and every day is a struggle just to get people to see me. Reach for the heavens? I'm busy trying to stay upright on the ground.

I want jazz band, and I want a job to buy a real trumpet to play in jazz band, and I want my parents to see me play and see how good I am and let me do music as a job and not a hobby, and I want, and I want, and I want until I'm breathless and starving from all the wanting.

"Come on." He pulls my hand.

The trumpet he shows me is the stuff of dreams. A 1923 Faciebat Anno Stradivarius. Engraved flowers and leaves etch the gold frame.

"Family heirloom," he says, which tells me everything I need to know about its cost. "Wanna hold it?"

I shake my head. It would be like touching the upper stratosphere. How would I come down after that? How would I hold and love Georgia, after that? I trace the round lines of the bell with my finger. "Thanks," I tell him when I find my voice. "It's beautiful." We turn to leave when I see it. Not the stuff of dreams. The stuff of life and breath. It's like a sudden spotlight is on the trumpet, and its lines and curves hit me like a physical punch to the gut.

Gold valves and a main tuning slide that's alternating blocks of silver and gold. But the bell. Copper that's been polished and hewn, so it's not so much copper but pale pink.

"Like it?" He asks.

"Is there a discount on instruments if you work here?"

"Yeah."

"If I worked here, that would make this—"

"A couple of thousand instead of a few thousand. But there are other trumpets you could start with, less expensive, you know?"

Less expensive, more expensive. None of it matters. I get thirty dollars a month for chores. My savings account has a few hundred dollars, and that's for university. It'll take me decades to get a down payment.

"You sure you don't know enough about music? I could put in a good word with Masao. . . ."

"Thanks for letting me look at them." I head for the door, but in my daydreams, I'm back at the store, buying a trumpet with the money from a part-time job. A breath later, my mind's eye has taken me to center stage, where I wail and play to an adoring crowd. My parents are in the audience, proud, not horrified, that their daughter is a musician.

"You need anything? New mouthpiece? Oil?"

"How soon do you think that job will be filled?" I come to a stop by the cash register. Behind me, I hear the tinkle of the bell as someone enters the store. I'm too busy calculating the odds of achieving my dreams to turn around and look.

"It's been up for a couple of months." He peers at me as though trying to figure out my secret. "Masao would take any recommendation I give him."

"Hey, Nira."

My mouth's suddenly dry at the familiar voice. It wasn't just a random someone who came into the store. It was the ultimate someone. I turn to face Noah.

"I'll tell Masao to look out for you. He'll be back in town in a couple of weeks."

"Okay, thanks." I wheeze the words, my gaze still locked on Noah. I'm hoping I look mildly surprised at his appearance. Smart money's on me looking like a turkey who's just woken up on the slaughter line.

Noah smiles. "What're you doing here?"

I'm still grappling with the fact he knows my name. Noah knows my name. Sure, theories of a multiverse say there must be a parallel universe where he knows my name. But I never figured it would be this universe. Where he knows my name. Noah knows my name.

"What is it? Top secret or something?"

And the question makes me realize I've been standing there, mouth wide open, with the loop *he knows my name, he knows my name* echoing in my head. "Uh, no, not top secret."

"We were looking at trumpets and maybe having her work here." Alec smiles at me as though he's being helpful.

Next visit, he and I are going to have a long talk where I explain that customer service doesn't mean telling people my business.

"I didn't know you play the trumpet," says Noah.

"What do you know about me?" I blurt the question, then go back to looking like a dumbstruck turkey.

He grins. "Nothing else, okay, Super Spy?"

"You here for strings?"

It takes me a second to realize Alec's talking to Noah.

"Yeah." Noah's face folds into a scowl. "Broke another one. So, if you play trumpet, does that mean you're trying out for jazz band?"

"Huh? Oh, uh, yeah." I'd say yes to anything if it meant he'd keep talking to me.

"So, what do you play?" He clasps my wrist and nudges me in the direction of the guitar accessories.

"Trumpet."

He grins. "I know that. I meant, which kind? B-flat? Bass, cornet?"

My brain's as empty as a dust bowl. I'm ninety percent positive if I tell him I play a much-loved but banged-up pocket trumpet some guy donated to Goodwill a billion years ago, he's going to stop talking to me.

"Okay, Super Spy," he says with a laugh when I stay quiet. "Keep your secrets. Come on, help me buy a string."

"I don't know anything about—" Shut up, Nira. Shut up. I smile. "Sure."

CHAPTER FOUR

HOPE IS A HIGH-CALORIE SWEETENER

The meeting for jazz band happens during lunch. There are about thirty kids who want to try out. Just my luck, McKenzie's one of them.

"Why are you here?" she asks. "This isn't science club or mathletics."

"Thanks, I didn't realize that—"

Emily comes up beside me. She's my curvy conscience whose presence shuts my mouth before I say something rude.

McKenzie stares a little too long at her. "Why are you here?"

Man, I want to punch her. "What are you? The band police?"

"I'm just asking—"

"Why are you here?" I ask. "What can you play?" Other than my last nerve.

"Saxophone," she says. "Alto sax."

"Hey, Super Spy."

Noah comes up, smiles at me, at McKenzie and Emily, and the urge to smack down McKenzie melts in the heat of his proximity. Noah is talking to me. In public. The most popular guy in school is acknowledging my presence.

"Come to show us how it's done?"

I babble a response, then I'm saved by the entrance of Mr. Nam. He gives us the rundown, and it's all routine—practice times, commitment, events—until he says, "Because of budget cuts, you will be responsible for bringing your own instrument."

I'm screwed. I can't walk into the audition with Georgia. I'll get laughed out of the room. Especially with McKenzie there. Plus, Georgia. He's an inanimate object, but he's real to me and I don't want to set him up for ridicule. I feel my dream evaporating into nothing but I won't let it disappear.

I have to get a job. God, what am I thinking? Ask permission for a part-time job, from my parents? I have a better chance of discovering a planet where unicorns and gummy bears coexist.

"This is cool," says Noah, nudging my arm. "You and I will get to play together."

"Huh?"

"Noah always gets in," says McKenzie. She bumps him with her shoulder and gives him a special smile. "He's amazing."

When he laughs and shakes his head, there's no false modesty.

He's genuinely pleased by her compliment. "So is she." He gestures to McKenzie. "She can make that sax wail."

I'm not surprised. God knows she makes me wail. "That's great that you guys are shoo-ins for the band," I tell him, "but I still have to try out."

"For you, that's just paperwork," says Noah. "If your playing is anything like your marks in school, you'll be leading the band."

McKenzie doesn't look happy about that. She shifts closer to Noah. "What kind of instrument do you play?"

"Trumpet."

"What kind?"

"A B-flat trumpet."

"Yeah, but what brand? Bach, Yamaha, Jupiter?"

Trust her to ask about the brand name. I'm saved by Mr. Nam shooting us a glare.

"As I was saying"—he pauses to give me the fish eye—"try-outs will happen in two weeks. You must be prepared to practice on your own time. Practice here means jamming and figuring out the blend, not figuring out your fingering or what notes come after what notes. You slack off, you're out. We've got a tight performance schedule, not to mention the city and regional finals."

"How grumpy is this guy?" asks Emily.

"It's not his fault," says Noah, "not really. His wife's in the hospital, some kind of complication with her pregnancy."

"Oh." Emily's eyes go soft. "That's so sad."

"Am I interrupting something?" Mr. Nam shoots another glare in our direction.

I shake my head.

"Don't worry about it," Noah whispers. "He's a s'more. Crunchy on the outside, but soft filling."

I'm not worried. Mr. Nam may be a s'more, but my parents are overbaked cookies. Hard all the way through. I can meet anything he sets out.

What I'm worried about is the timing of the audition and the need to get a new instrument. How can I get a job, get paid, and get a trumpet before practice? And how will I convince my parents that I can hold down a part-time job, keep up my marks, and find time for practice and night events?

---◇---

When I get off the bus and start for home, I'm hungry for food. But I want the trumpet from Reynolds so badly, I can taste the metal on my tongue. Hunger is making me stupid and lustful for all the things I can't have. And it's growing, taking me over. I'm famished for a million things, and none of them is within my grasp. The trumpet. A place in jazz band. Noah as a friend. Clothes. I want it all. I want it now. And I have just low enough blood sugar to delude me into believing I can convince my parents to give me permission.

I head up the sidewalk to my house and reality reasserts its ugly, low-calorie, no fat, no sugar head. How can I ask my parents for permission to get a job? When I placed second in that stupid science contest, they pulled all the specialty channels from our cable package because they said it was distracting me.

Even Georgia. I had to haggle with them like a SWAT team negotiator just to get permission to buy him. The only reason I got him was because I did a butt load of extra credit projects and was the first kid in the elementary school history to graduate grade three with an average that exceeded a hundred percent.

The trumpet was a gift, but my parents nixed the idea of lessons. Georgia was for playtime, when I was done with my home-work, and they weren't going to spend money on trivialities. Not when they were saving for my doctoral degree so I can cure cancer, the water crisis, and static cling, and do it all before I'm thirty-five.

I had one brief, shining moment of possibility when my ele-mentary school started a band course. Unfortunately for me, the practice time for band conflicted with the math club. My parents nixed my request. I tried begging, but when that risked getting Georgia taken away from me, I opted for learning to play via the online videos. And even then, any *real* playing I do is when Mom and Dad aren't home. They don't know how good I truly am, they don't know about how I mix music and melody. Why would I share? They would dismiss it, and I love music and my trumpet too much to expose them to the light of my parents' disdain.

I try to hold my temper as these memories surge, but they're raising my heart rate. Why does it always have to be a battle with them? I head up the steps to the house.

As I put the key in the lock and turn the knob, I hear it. They're arguing. About what I don't know. I creep inside and hang my coat. They're in the bedroom, behind the closed door.

I kick off my shoes and sneak into the kitchen. Grandma is there, knitting. The kettle's bubbling on the counter. After I wash my hands, I sit by her. "Can I help with something?"

She shakes her head. "You want tea?"

My mother's voice pitches high. My father's roars in response.

"Trade you some tea for earplugs."

She sets down the fluff of yarn, and I take her hand. And squeeze it when the bedroom door flies open.

"When you went out, did you see the leaves changing color?" she asks. "It was beautiful. Next time, come with me. We'll look at them together."

"How about now? Let's run away from these insane people. We'll hop on a train and see the world." I hold up my phone. "I've got the health app with all of your medications, the files for your estate. Give me the word and I'll download your bank's app. We'll run away to Paris."

The kettle bubbles and clicks off. "Tea first." Grandma rises.

I gently push her back down, then move to the counter.

"You always do this! Always!" My father's steps falter when he sees us, then speed up again as he heads through the kitchen to the basement stairs.

"What is always?" Mom yells back. Her hands are up and close to her chest. Pleading or protecting her heart, I can't tell. "I thought it would be nice."

"It's not nice; it's cheap! Why do you always have to be impatient?"

"Again, with the always! I thought it would be nice!"

Mom and Dad are repeating themselves, and the clues aren't enough to put together the puzzle.

I glance at my grandmother, but she's not saying anything. Drives me crazy. She knows what's going on—she always knows what's going on. When it comes to family matters and secrets, she's a brown and wrinkled Deep Throat.

Dad veers away from the stairs, pushes past my mother. A few seconds later, I hear the slam of the front door. Then the screech of the engine firing to life. The kitchen is silent. Mom stands frozen at the fridge. Grandma's knitting, but her needles make no sound.

Mom's eyes slide to me, and it's like she's seeing me for the first time.

I shrink against the counter and hope she thinks I'm a teapot cozy.

"Nira, come help me."

Double shrink. When she's really mad, her voice is calm and low. That's hide-the-knives mad and talk-her-down-with-tea-fudge-and-mithai mad. "Okay. Do you want some tea?"

"No."

The look Grandma shoots me is a total go with God.

I frown at her because I don't understand why she's giving me that look and I wish she'd open her mouth. "Sure. Do you need me to bring anything?"

"Matches."

Oh, jeez.

The matches, thank god, are not to burn down the house or any of Dad's possessions. They're for the small camping BBQ sitting by the house, under the kitchen window. "Oh, it's cute."

"Your father," she spits the words. "Why does he have to be like that?"

"Stubborn? Dictatorial? Recalcitrant?"

"Eh, don't vex me. Now's not the time to prove your vocabulary." She hefts a bag of charcoal and rips it open with her bare hands.

I step out of her range and go with the instinctual, "Sorry."

"Why does he have to be like that?"

I hold the metal grill as she tosses the bricks into the black bin.

No point in talking to her when she's on the repetitive loop.

"Is it so bad? Tell me, is it so bad?" She wrenches the grill from my hand, and I thank any gods in the vicinity for saving me from a broken finger. Or three.

"No, it's not so bad." Safe response.

"I know." She tosses a lit match on the charcoal and watches the embers burn out. "But he's so—"

I don't offer any synonyms and hope she'll put me out of my misery by telling me what it is they're fighting about.

She lights another match. "What is so bad with making do?"

I'm lost.

"What's the big deal if we can't afford that gargantuan BBQ like Raj?"

Oh.

"What's wrong with having a little one like this?" She waves at the grill with the slick motion of a professional model. "Who cares what it looks like? What matters is what it cooks like. And charcoal is charcoal. It all tastes the same."

"Right." I'm glad Dad's not here to see another match burn out without having lit the charcoal. He'd lecture us for days on how it's proof the BBQ is crap. "I'm on your side, but we're still without a fire in the grill."

"It needs help. Get me some newspaper."

But that doesn't work. Neither do the white blocks of whatever that is she shoves between the bricks. As she works, she complains about Dad.

"I know we have to save for some things. But not everything—not everything has to have a brand name and a big price tag. Sometimes the no name is just as good."

I disagree, but I need her on my side.

"You don't care." Another match dies. "You and your designer jeans."

"That's not fair," I tell the back of her as she turns and bends toward a plastic bag. "Just because I like brand names doesn't mean I can't understand where you're coming from. Some things are—" She whips out a bag with the ferocity of a Samurai wielding a sword. "What the—?"

She's pulled out a giant bottle of lighter fluid. "I'm tired of your dad telling me I'm bad for not wanting to wait on every little thing. Why can't we have fun with what we have?" As she's talking, she's spraying the charcoal with fluid. The more she talks, the harder she pushes on the bottle.

"Mom, I think that's enough."

"It is enough, Nira. I'm not letting him talk to me like that anymore—"

"I mean, there's going to be a fire."

"Don't be so dramatic. Your father and I aren't going to self-destruct."

"No, I mean the—"

"I'll show him." Another squirt of fluid on the BBQ. "I'll prove to him this thing's just as good as Raj's Colossus." Another shot on the charcoal. "You can do a lot with a little."

I grab the bottle out of her hand.

"Look at you with your toy trumpet."

Uh-oh.

"Listen to the great music you play, even though it's not expensive or pretty to look at. You do a great job. You don't need anything else."

Outstanding. Just what I least needed to hear.

"It's what you said. With some things, you don't need to spend hundreds or get a brand name."

I eye the bottle in my hand and consider dousing myself with it. "But some things, quality things, you need to spend money."

"Nira." Her impatient gaze rubs me like sandpaper. "Are you with me or not?"

"I'm with both of you."

"You can't be with both of us."

"Why not?"

"Because one of us is wrong." Another glare. "And I'm the one who gave birth to you."

Ugh. Parents. "You can prove your point with the food."

"Go get me the chicken."

"Stop drowning the bricks with lighter fluid."

When I come back, I see her sprinkling the bricks with the liquid. "What did I say about the fluid?" I set down the dish of chicken legs. "With the amount you've sprayed—" Then I remember I'm supposed to have her onside. "Can I help?"

"I'll start it, then you can watch it while I make the potatoes." She reaches for the matches. "Unless you want to peel them?"

No, no, and more no. All I'll hear is how I peel too thick and need to cut more of the eyes out. "I'll watch."

With a flick of her wrist, the match flames to life. Another flick, and it's spiraling through the air and touches the bricks. There's a loud *foom*, an apocalyptic cloud of smoke and flame, and black clouds explode to the sky.

A second later, as the haze clears, the fire's burning with cheerful orange and red in the BBQ. Our eyes travel upward, tracking the path of soot that's been licked into the white wall.

"You still have that twenty? The one I gave you for your jeans?"

"Yeah."

"Go get paint. And a brush."

"He's going to be home soon. The store's a half hour away."

She turns to the chicken. "Run."

I don't get back in time, and dinner's full of unspoken words. The weird thing is that each of my parents thinks they've won the argument. Dad looks self-satisfied because of the swatch of black on the exterior of our house. Mom's smug because the chicken is deliciousness itself.

Grandma eats. I wonder how she can be so placid, but I guess if she survived raising Dad and Uncle Raj, nothing can phase her. After dinner, I help with the dishes. When I go outside, I find Dad in the backyard, staring at the cloud of doom left by the BBQ. He shakes his head when he sees me. "Your mother. Why can't she wait?"

"Because if you look up 'impatient' in the dictionary, there's a picture of her."

He grunts. "Look at this. We'll have to scrape the paint, then put more on. And you know what'll happen? It's going to look terrible because it'll be brand-new and the rest of the house is old white. We're going to have to paint the entire wall. Maybe the entire house."

I'm still stuck on "we." "We?"

"Yes, Nira. You helped her."

"Helped! I was trying to talk her off the ledge."

"Good." He nods. "Then you'll help."

"I—" Why am I fighting this? I can flip being a good daughter into a negotiation for the trumpet and the jazz band. "Fine, I'll help."

His focus is on the wall, and he looks like he's trying not to cry. "I don't know how we'll afford all the paint and the equipment. This is hundreds of dollars of damage."

I'm tempted to twist his words, to point out that if I had a job, I could help with the money. But he's in a fragile state, and I worry about his reaction.

He's still staring at the wall. The setting sun casts its orange-red light and imbues the house with shades of underworld chic. "What's so bad with having some patience?"

"I guess you miss stuff if all you do is wait."

"Of course, you agree with her." He gives himself a shake, and the father I know—staid, implacable—reemerges.

"What? No. I'm just saying I understand why she wants to do stuff now. Just like I understand why you'd want to wait. Some things—quality things—you have to save up for."

He nods, satisfied.

"We're a lot alike," I tell him. I smile for emphasis and hope I don't look like a slimy saleslady. "We have an idea of the kind of life we want, and we don't mind working hard to get it."

Another nod. And a smile.

"Dad"—I take a breath to quiet my increasing heart rate, which is one beat below a heart attack—"I want something."

"The clothes? Not again—"

"No, no. Something else. Something . . . big." Before he can say anything, my mouth gets ahead of my brain. "It's not school related, so I don't expect you to shell out the money. I want an after-school job to pay for it."

He doesn't reply, only stares.

I've never been in a hurricane before, but I think this is what it must be like. People talk about the hush when you're in the middle of the storm, but it's not an accurate word. There's no hush between Dad and me. It's a lack of sound that's loud and thunderous in its silence, and it's making my ears pound.

"You want a what?" He asks the question like I've not only confessed to being pregnant but admitted that the father in question is Satan and my child will bring about the end times.

"I want a job, to save up for something."

"What kind of something?"

He's talking without moving his lips, and it's freaking me out. "It's—"

"You're saving money?" He steps closer. "Is this for a boy?"

"You can't buy people anymore, Dad. Besides, brown folks owning other folks will cause talk in the neighborhood."

"Don't get fresh. You know what I mean. You saving up for something you want to do with a boy?"

I shake my head.

His eyes narrow. "Or a girl? Don't play word games with me, Nira. Boy, girl. You know what I'm asking. Are you doing things you're not supposed to be doing?"

"Of course not! When do I have the time to do anything other than study? I'm not saving up to do anything with anyone." That's not true. Playing the trumpet would be even cooler if there were other instruments. My thoughts must show on my face because my dad's eyes go snaky.

"Safiya! Come here! Your daughter's eyes pass me."

Why does everything have to be so hard with them? Trust him to see my expression and misread it.

Mom shushes us as she comes out the door. "It's getting late. You want to get the neighbors mad?"

"Tell her. Tell her what's so important you need a job—"

"A job!" She says it like I've cussed at her. "School is your job."

"—to save up. For something personal."

"Is it a boy?"

"I'm not buying—no."

Her dark eyes probe my face. "A girl?"

"No."

"What is it for?"

"It's something I want."

"More clothes?" She steps closer to Dad.

"She'd tell us if it were clothes." He closes the space between them.

Boy, nothing like a kid asking for something to make parents forget their fight and bond together.

"You're sure you're not dating? Have you been lying to us about the bus ride? You've been going somewhere to meet someone?"

"No, no." Dad claps his hands. "Hear the joke. She's too busy to date, she has no time after she's done studying, but somehow, she's going to find time for a job."

"It's a trumpet." I blurt the words out before I can process my thoughts.

They stare, as though I've spoken in Russian. As though I've grown another head, and it's speaking Russian, too.

"Trumpet?" says my mother. "What's wrong with the one you have?"

"It's a pocket trumpet, it's not the standard size for band."

"It's almost as big as a real trumpet—"

"I love—" I almost say "Georgia," but stop myself in time. My parents don't need to know I've named my trumpet. "I love my trumpet, but it's a hundred years old."

"Why do you need a new one?"

"Why does Dad need a BBQ? We have a stove."

"Eh, don't get fresh."

Right, I'm disrespectful for pointing out the obvious.

Mom rolls her eyes. "Like the jeans. Always want, want, want."

I exhale my angry breath. "That's why I'd like a job. Because then it's my money and I can spend it on anything I want." Whoa. Dumb thing to say.

They take a synchronous step my way. "On anything you want."

"Is this about drugs?" asks Dad. "Are you experimenting?"

"Is this about The Pot?"

God help me. How do two adults who come from a country where marijuana is considered a staple call it The Pot? "No."

"We didn't come here for you to fry your brain on Canadian grass. This isn't like the ganja from back home—"

"I just want a trumpet."

There's a long look between them where they communicate telepathically. Who knows, maybe they even contact the mother ship. Then they speak with one voice. "No."

"What!"

"No," says my dad. "You have to go to school. That's your job."

"But it doesn't pay!" The wind picks up and blows cold kisses on the back of my neck.

"But it will," says Mom. "When you go to university and become a neurosurgeon."

"I don't want to be a neurosurgeon."

She waves her hand, dismisses me. "Fine. Fine. Be a heart surgeon. Plastic surgeon. General surgeon. Any kind of surgeon you want. It's your life."

"Yeah, right." My words are bitter. "That's why I'm begging for permission to have an after-school job. My marks are great. What's the big deal if I work part-time?"

"Your marks will drop. We didn't come here for you to end up in a gutter."

"God, Dad! Who are these kids that end up in the gutter? I'm a good kid—"

"And you'll stay that way if you stay in school."

"It's part of the Canadian experience." I'm growing desperate. "Don't you want me to be Canadian?"

"Not that Canadian," says Mom. "Besides, who will take you to this job?"

"The bus," I tell her.

"More time wasted," she says. "You're riding the bus when you should be studying."

"I can study on the bus."

"With all that noise and people breathing beside you?" Her eyebrows go up.

"Trust me," I tell her. "As long as they're breathing, I'm fine. It's the guy beside me who's not breathing who's going to worry me."

"Fresh," mutters Dad. "You see what happens when we let her watch those stupid shows on TV?"

All this, just because I want something that doesn't have a direct connection to academics. Last year, I tried to convince them that I should have more than school courses on my résumé. They were willing to bend for me for volunteering at a hospital or a vet clinic. But when I asked about music, they built a wall that would have made Shihuangdi jealous, which is saying a lot, since he built the Great Wall of China. In my parents' world, the arts have no place except as an excuse for those who don't want "real" jobs.

"You're shivering." Mom rubs my arm. "Let's go inside and discuss this." She drops her voice and whispers, "Away from the neighbors."

"No one's pressed up against their kitchen window, Mom." I can't keep the sarcasm out of my voice. "Me wanting a trumpet isn't that interesting."

"It is to me." She beams a smile.

Shoot me.

"We'll go in and talk."

"No." I'm such an idiot. Why not say okay and go inside? My fingers are turning to brown icicles, and my boobs are so cold my nipples are going to shatter.

"Nira, we didn't raise you to pout and throw tantrums. You want this, come inside and talk to us like an adult."

Song number two on the Ghani family playlist. Look like a child, act like a grown-up. Talk like an adult, think like an adult, make decisions like an adult. I have all the responsibilities and obligations of the graying crowd without any of the privileges. "Not until you agree."

"You're going to stay outside until we let you have a trumpet?"

I nod.

They shrug. "Okay," and go inside.

The kitchen light comes on. Warm yellow spills onto the concrete. I sit on the tree stump and wrap my arms around myself as the sun sets and the dark creeps in. A few minutes later, Grandma's beside me, a cup of tea in her hand.

"How much for the trumpet?"

"A lot." I take the cup from her and swallow a mouthful of sweet tea. It burns my mouth, scalds my throat, but I don't care. It's hot, and I need it. And at least this time it's not so sweet it'll put me in a diabetic coma. My stomach blooms with its warmth. "I need the job because I can't save it up."

"Maybe I can help."

Tears sting my eyes. "It's too much."

"Maybe I can help."

I shake my head.

"They only want what's best for you."

"No, they don't. They want me to live their dream. Science. Math. Grow up to be a doctor. I don't want any of it. I don't want to cut into anybody." Not that I don't want to touch people's hearts— I just want to do it differently. But I need courage and confidence. And I need magic for that. Magic is the trumpet.

"They sacrificed so you could have a better life—"

"What kind of life? I'm the only brown girl in school. The only other brown kid is some guy in the next grade. And he's actual brown, full Indian, not some weird mix of a bunch of races, like me."

"It's not a weird mix. It's exotic ethnicities—"

"That no one cares about except you."

She clasps my hand, and her skin is as cold as mine.

I wrap my fingers around her to warm her up.

"It's not about what you look like and who else looks like you. It's about opportunity and taking your chances in this country."

"You don't understand. It's not like home."

"Home is poverty. People were lining up for milk, Nira."

"Yeah, but everyone is poor there. You don't have anything, but who cares, because no one else has anything, either. Here, you don't have stuff, but the other guy, he has everything. And no one understands why you don't have the same food like them. Or, when they want to go to a movie or eat out, you can't go because you don't have the money for it."

"Nira—"

But I don't want to hear it. I shake my head, and the silence slips between us. She frees her hand, pats my lap. With a grunt, she's on her feet and walking back to the house. I want to call her back, to take back what I've said. But it would be a lie, and I've never lied to my grandma.

It only takes a few seconds for my anger to cool, then I'm nothing but the idiot brown girl, sitting alone in the dark and freezing her butt off.

A few seconds later, she's in front of the window, standing by the sink.

Mom comes up to her. Gestures to where I sit.

Grandma speaks.

Mom argues. Hands up, hands out.

Grandma speaks again.

More hands.

Grandma.

Mom, hands down, ear cocked. Walks away.

Five minutes, ten. I hold the cup until the lingering heat from the ceramic is absorbed into my skin.

Mom comes out. "I have your jacket, but if you come inside, we can talk about it."

"Talk? Or you just tell me what I can do and what I can have."

"Talk. Promise.'"

When I get into the kitchen, there are four cups and a teapot stacked by the boiling kettle. "I'll make the tea."

"I can do it," says Grandma. "You talk to your parents."

Mom gets Dad from the bedroom, then the three of us sit around the table. Dad's anger radiates from him like static electricity. Mom looks disappointed in me. And I want to cry.

I live in a world where the TV and movies show me happy families and parents who talk to their kids and try to understand their point of view. The kids at school have parents who backpacked through Europe or experimented with drugs. Their folks drank in the dorms and shacked up with poor life-mate choices. Canada is like this multicolored tapestry, where a parent's life and a kid's come together to make this amazing image.

But my life's not like that. My address may be in Canada, but I live in little Guyana, a benevolent dictatorship where I'm not a full citizen. The number-one rule here is to obey your elders. The number-two rule is to check your individuality at the door. This is a community, one organism with a bunch of parts, and we rise and fall together.

Mom and Dad have never defied their parents. It would never occur to them that me having my own opinion isn't rebellion. They grew up poor. They look at my wanting stuff like I'm spitting in the face of their sacrifices, and nothing I do seems to change their minds.

"This job," my mother starts the conversation as Grandma drops the tea bags into the pot. "Where are you going to work?"

"I don't know yet."

Dad snorts.

"I don't know yet because I didn't want to get too far into researching places without having your permission."

He huffs, but his shoulders drop a few inches.

"And you want this job because you want to buy a trumpet?" asks my mom. "It's that important to you?"

I nod.

"We can get it for you," she says. "I don't like the idea of you working when you should be studying."

"It's too expensive for you to buy it for me." I smile at Grandma as she puts the teapot on the table and pours out a cup for each of us. "I don't understand why you're making a big deal about this. Keeping me focused on school isn't preparing me for living on my own as an adult."

Dad smirks. "But letting you gallivant around and buy clothes—"

"Letting me learn how to schedule my life when there's more than one thing is what's important," I say. "What happens when I'm married with kids and a job? If I don't learn how to juggle multiple things now, you think I'm miraculously going to learn it overnight?"

That makes Mom pause. She reaches for the mug Grandma sets before her.

Grandma puts my cup in front of me, and I catch the small smile at the edge of her mouth. She squeezes my shoulder.

I take a sip. There are only two teaspoons of sugar in the drink. That's a good sign. It means she doesn't think this discussion will cause the end of the world.

"But why do you need a new one? The old one is fine," says Dad.

"That's what I told you when you wanted a new bike," Grandma tells him.

His face screws up. He takes the mug from her hands. "It's not the same thing. That bike was for work. I was a messenger, and the chain on the old one broke all the time. She's not doing anything with the trumpet." He takes a sip, grimaces, and ladles another spoon of sugar into his cup.

Grandma nods at his words, and Dad shoots me a look of victory.

"You're right," says Grandma. "She needs to do something with the trumpet. Nira, didn't you say the school was holding jazz band auditions?"

The table freezes into a stop-motion tableau. Our faces are caught in the moment—Mom, shock. Dad looks like the betrayal will become a generational grudge. I'm sure my expression mirrors a mongoose in the crosshairs of a snake.

"Nira," Grandma says, "fetch the flyer."

I don't know what to do. I'm locked in a combination of delight that she's doing this and terror of being grounded until I die.

"Fetch!" Grandma barks, and I jump from my seat and scurry to my room.

When I return, they're still staring at each other. The only thing moving is the rising steam from the cups. I hold out the flyer. No one takes it. I let it fall to the table.

"Now a job and band?" Dad asks. He drains his cup and refills it.

"Is that so bad?" Grandma pushes the sugar bowl his way. "You did it as a child."

"It was different then," he says.

"How?" She speaks softly, but there's a challenge in her voice. It's the same challenge I hear in my parents—the one only a mom or dad can use on their kid.

"Because—"

"Yes, of course." Grandma nods as though she's answered the question herself. "School here is different than back home. Harder—"

Dad makes a sound of exquisite contempt. "Here? Give me a break. Canadian kids have it so easy. They don't even know how to add sums in their head!" His chest puffs out. "Guyana's education is top-notch. What I was learning at Nira's age, the kids here learn in university!"

"If it's not the school work, then it must be Nira," says Grandma. "She's not smart like Farah—"

"She's smarter than Farah!"

Mom and I watch, dumbfounded. Grandma's a Guyanese Geppetto, and she's pulling Dad's strings like a master puppeteer.

"Then she can't be trusted with the responsibility," Grandma says it with a note of finality, and the curtain goes down on my hope.

"Exactly," says Dad.

"I've talked to you, over and over, about how you raise the picknie."

My ears perk at the word. Picknie, it's an affectionate term for a child. Grandma hasn't deserted me, yet.

"You train a child in the way they go. If she's not responsible, that's your fault."

Anger flashes in Dad's eyes. "She's plenty responsible. I know how to raise my picknie!"

"Good." Grandma smiles and takes a slow sip of her tea. "Then she'll get the job and apply for band."

Dad goes slack in stunned silence. Mom's eyes dart between her husband and her mother-in-law.

I choke back my laughter, but I'm too ecstatic to contain myself, and the sound comes out as a squeak.

Grandma, the puppet master, rises and I'm quick to follow. No need to sit here and risk Dad rallying the second round.

"Safiya." She sashays out of the kitchen. "I liked the chicken. It tasted much better than the one Gul and Raj cooked on that monstrosity of a BBQ."

My mother perks up. I want to kneel before my grandmother and beg her to teach me everything she knows about negotiating and manipulating. I hazard a peek at my parents as I leave the kitchen. Mom's drinking her tea, a soft smile on her lips. Dad's staring into the mouth of his cup, muttering to himself. No doubt trying to figure out how an octogenarian just bested him. I steal into my room, my steps made easy and light by the victory at my feet.

CHAPTER FIVE

FORTUNE IS A
TWO-HEADED SNAKE

"**W**here are you going to work?" Emily asks as we sit in the cafeteria, watching life pass by us. The lunch special is pizza, and the scent of pepperoni and mozzarella makes my processed cheese sandwich even more pathetic. I've tried to up its cool factor with a side of fries, but it's a lost cause.

Reynolds crosses my mind, but the fact Mom and Dad said yes means I need to move. Fast. Waiting and studying for a job gives the parentals time to change their mind. "I don't know. Anywhere that will take me, I guess." My gaze drifts to the popular table. I wish they would take me. I jerk my chin at them and ask Emily. "Do you ever wish we had more cred with them?"

She watches them.

"They don't see us." I feel like an idiot, stating the obvious. "Doesn't that make you feel—"

Emily nods. "Yeah, whenever I think about them, I feel invincible."

"You mean invisible."

"Invincible. If they can't see me, they can't stop me."

I don't know what I ever did to get a friend like her, but I have to figure out the answer so I can keep doing it and keep her with me.

She clamps down on my arm. "We should."

"We should what?" I ask, even though I know what she's saying. "Learn the two-step? Fly to Mars? Do whatever it is you want because we're the Invincible Invisibles?"

"Go to the mall and hand out résumés."

"You say it like you're looking for a job."

She shrugs. "Extra money doesn't hurt."

"Please. You have a live-in housekeeper and cook. What do you need money for?"

Her eyes go dreamy. "I want to find a forbidden love and run away to a foreign land with her."

"Anna Karenina tried that with her lover," I tell her. "It didn't end well."

Emily takes a bite of her hoagie. "So, this Anna chick," she says around a mouthful of salami and veggies. "She goes to our school or something?"

I freeze, trying to figure out a way to tell her Anna's not a real person but a character in one of literature's great classics, and do it without making her feel stupid.

She laughs. "It's so easy to mess with you. I know it's a novel. Leo Tallboy."

"Tolstoy."

"You shouldn't be that easy to screw around with."

I punch her on the shoulder. "Thanks for getting me."

"Consider me the Jane Goodall of the neurotic brown girl tribe." She waggles her eyebrows and shoves a banana my way. "Huh? Huh?"

"You know that's vaguely racist—"

"Not all primates like bananas? Think I should shove some sprouted grains at you?"

I can't speak because I'm laughing too hard. She's such a dork, and I'm lucky to have her. McKenzie looks up. She's glowering at Emily, staring so hard, her gaze could laser through my friend's skull.

My cheeks heat. With anger. With shame. I shouldn't be embarrassed to have fun here. I shouldn't feel like I don't belong. I'm going to get a job and then I'm going to get a trumpet that's so great the rest of them can't even dream about it. My shoulders go back, and I glare at McKenzie, vibe the message I know who and what you are. Stay away from my friend. I'm shocked when her face colors and she ducks from my stare.

"Hey, Super Spy." Noah slides into the chair next to me, and the cafeteria takes a collective gasp. The murmurs start. I know why they're whispering. Why is he with them?

"What's up with that, anyway? Super Spy?" asks Emily.

"It's a long story," I say, and turn my back, so I don't have to see McKenzie.

"About a trumpet." Noah helps himself to my fries.

"Have you heard?" Emily asks.

"Heard her play?" Noah shakes his head. "Not yet."

Good god. He speaks Emily.

"You think it'll be easy for her to get into jazz band?" More fries disappear into his mouth. Which is just as well, because I'm too gobsmacked by what's going on to be hungry.

"Totally." Emily jabs me hard in the ribs. "I'm glad I'm not the only one who thinks you should try out."

"I haven't heard her play," says Noah.

"She's good enough to be lead. She's incredible, especially considering—"

I don't know if she's doing her psychic twin thing or if she's setting up the reveal that I play a pocket trumpet, but it's time to end their cozy time. A sharp elbow to her ribs stops her midsentence.

"Ah," says Noah. "The super spy appears. Are you going to tell us what you're playing for the audition, or is that classified?"

In the corner of my eye, I see McKenzie edging our way. I guess my glare wasn't enough to make her leave me alone on a permanent basis. "Did you come here to talk to me about music?"

He pushes my plate toward me. "Yes and no. I came here for another reason."

No wonder McKenzie's wriggling our way. Of course, he's here for something other than the joy of sitting with Emily and me. "What did you want?"

"Your forgiveness," he says.

Now I'm worried. "What did you do?"

McKenzie slides into the seat next to him, smiles, and rubs his arm.

"I told Alec he should push Masao hard to hire you," says Noah.

"You did?" It comes out as a squeak.

He nods. "You love that place, he told me so. Anyway—" He nudges me. "We musicians have to stick together."

Noah is on the front lines for me. I'm not stupid enough to read into it. Helping people is Noah's trademark; it's what he does. But the fact I made his radar, and he pushed his cred in my direction, is amazing. I put the job at Reynolds on the simmer setting in my brain. I'll need to learn about other instruments, and I don't know if I have time to do it—not while there's a ticking clock with my parents. But Noah's kindness leaves me dizzy.

This is all too much, and I need Hedi Lamar, Adriana Ocampo, and Marie Curie here. Noah Who Is So Cool He Needs No Last Name is sitting at my table. So is McKenzie King. If it wouldn't look super dorky, I'd take out my phone and check the compass to see if the poles have reversed themselves.

"The audition's coming up," he says, and brings me back to reality. "How's practice?"

"I'm going so hard at it." McKenzie rubs his arm, then wriggles closer to Emily as though that will cover her flirtation. "If I could be sax lead, that would be amazing."

Subtle. Noah said I could be lead, and suddenly, she wants it.

"You should see Alec this weekend and follow up," says Noah.

It takes me a second to focus on what he's talking about, and then I'm telepathically trying to get him to shut up, but it doesn't work. He's talking about the hours and store discounts, and it catches McKenzie's interest. Which means she's suddenly asking what's going on, and he's telling her, and now she knows I need money. And the whole time they're talking, she keeps touching him, like somehow if she stops, he'll disappear from existence.

"We're going to the mall to hand out résumés," says Emily. "But now maybe we don't have to—"

"We should still go," I tell her. "Nothing's nothing until it's something."

"Cool. Both of you are looking?"

Emily answers "yes" for us, and that's great because I'm too busy calculating how long it will take McKenzie to rub a hole into Noah's skin. Which makes me feel like a giant loser. I don't like Noah, not like that. I'm not even sure I like him as a friend. Sure, he's been nice so far. But I've gotten third-degree burns from people who seem nice. And for sure, I've known a lot of good-looking people who spray locusts every time they open their mouths. Like Farah and her parents. I'm just pissed that McKenzie can't let Emily and me have this moment with him.

"Mind if I tag along?" asks Noah. "I wouldn't mind getting a part-time gig."

"We should all go." McKenzie shoots him a smile and slides her snake eyes in Emily's direction.

I know she's judging my friend, judging the extra pounds and the extra chocolate on her plate, and it takes everything in me not to tell McKenzie off.

"I have to print off my résumé, so . . ." I can't believe I'm pulling an Emily, but there it is. Me, trailing off with the sentence and hoping they catch the hint.

"No problem," says Noah. "What if we went tomorrow?"

Either he didn't catch the hint, or he caught it and returned it with a curve ball.

"After school," adds McKenzie.

Emily agrees for both of us, and before I can even comprehend what's happened, I'm suddenly star of the weirdest teen movie, ever. Nira, The Girl Who Would Be Cool. The warning pings at the back of my mind.

I've been invisible since always. Something apocalyptic is going to happen—there's got to be a dark agenda behind McKenzie and Noah suddenly paying attention to me. Well, maybe not Noah. But McKenzie, definitely. But popular kids exude a kind of seductive pheromone, and I'm going under. I know I'm getting myself into trouble, but I can't stop myself from going along with them.

The next day, I spend most of my time scrolling through the possible scenarios for what will happen at the mall. If we even get to the mall. Maybe it's a prank of some kind. Emily and I will get to the spot, but Noah and McKenzie won't show. Instead, there'll be a hidden camera, videoing how long it takes us to realize we've been stood up.

I can't believe Noah would be mean, but he's with McKenzie, and she can be an idiot. I'm so caught up in my spy games, I barely register the A-minus on my chemistry exam. For sure, I'll get it from Dad, but that's the least of my concerns. I stuff the paper in my bag and go back to figuring out Noah and McKenzie's motivations.

I'm shocked as all get-out when the end of the day comes, and I find Noah at my locker, waiting with McKenzie and Emily.

We head to the mall, and after a half hour of random wandering, I decide whatever villainous deed they may have planned for us won't happen today.

I'm happy to be around them, but I hate it, too. I had a plan of the stores I'd approach. Nothing super high end or expensive. Those stores have a certain look to their employees, and it's a look I don't have.

Their staff have the right clothes, sleek hair, polished nails, and immaculate makeup. I have . . . none of those things. Forget about the clothes. And my hair is ethnic. It's in a perpetual state of frizz and dry, and Mom refuses to buy me the right kind of product. I try, but they're expensive. One bottle and I'm bankrupt for a month. Plus, I'm too intimidated to walk into a store selling jeans for a hundred dollars and ask for a job, when my jeans cost twenty-five dollars. It's like the pauper wanting to sit in the king's seat.

But for McKenzie, Emily, and Noah, these stores aren't foreign lands. They're a second home, familiar as an old couch. I'm left to follow and hand in my résumé and pretend as though I belong. And the weird thing is that when I'm with them, it's kind of like I do belong. They give me a strange legitimacy, and I don't know how I feel about that.

Part of me likes the feeling of belonging a little too much. It makes me feel heavy and light, all at the same time, and I bet that's what it feels like when you're drunk on something good. Most of me is angry that I can't be of value by myself. I'm just made visible because I'm with the others.

We get through half the stores in the mall before I run out of résumés. "We should celebrate a job well done," says McKenzie. "Let's grab some food. Oh, how about the fries place? The one that has all those crazy toppings."

And the crazy prices. A small order of fries from that place is twelve bucks. Add in a drink and—

"Oh, and cake from the bakery beside it," adds Emily.

—and there goes my money. I'm sweating as we head to the food court. I've never blown all my allowance at once, especially not on food. When all you get is thirty dollars, you make it last. That's why I never buy the expensive hair stuff, and I saved for two months to buy my cheap-ass jeans.

"Oh, wait." McKenzie pivots my way. "Can you eat that?"

"Fries? Yeah."

"But it'll have other stuff, like beef and—"

It takes everything in me not to shout at her. "I told you, I'm not Hindi. I can eat beef."

"But the meat won't be Hawaiian."

I'm dumbfounded. "What?"

"No," she says, "not Hawaiian, but it sounds like Hawaiian."

"Havarti?" suggests Noah.

"No, no." McKenzie shifts from one foot to the other, then back again. "It's like a religious thing."

"Hanukkah?" Emily offers.

McKenzie shakes her head. Her foot shuffling's increased, so now she looks like she's trying not to pee herself. "You know, meat religion."

I'm no longer dumfounded, but McKenzie is still dumb. "You mean halal."

She snaps her fingers. "Yeah, that's it! None of this stuff is hallelujah—hallamula—" She's flustered, her face flushes, and she opens her mouth to try again.

I raise my hand for her to stop. Not because I don't enjoy hearing her make an idiot of herself, but I'm afraid my muscles will act instinctually at the repetitious hacking of a religious tenet and I'll punch her. "I'm not Muslim; that's my aunt. I don't need the meat to be halal."

The food court is almost empty, so none of us needs to save a seat. As we wait, they talk about jazz band, but I'm not paying attention. I'm too busy trying to figure out a way to avoid spending all my money on food. When it's our turn, I tell them to go ahead because I'm still deciding. Emily wants butter chicken fries, Noah takes Philly cheese, and McKenzie has the same thing as Emily. When it's only me left to order, I tell the cashier all I want is a small pop.

"But you have to eat," says McKenzie.

Don't I know it. There are textbooks on the psychology and sociology of sharing a meal together and how it bonds people. It's been happening since the dawn of man, and for sure, eating is a big deal with this group. By not ordering I'm separating myself from them, and it's giving me hives. But this money needs to make it to the end of the month. Only, how can I say that to McKenzie, who always looks like her clothes came off the cover of a fashion magazine, Emily who has servants, and Noah who goes on exotic trips?

"I'm not hungry," I lie and hope my stomach doesn't growl.

"But the rest of us are eating," says McKenzie. "It'll be weird if you don't." Her mouth slackens, then, "Wait. Is this an eating disorder thing? I mean, do we need to have an intervention or something for you?"

"I'm not hungry."

"But you're kind of anorexic looking." McKenzie won't shut up. The glare I shoot her way makes her blush and drop her gaze.

"I've seen her eat." Emily smiles. "She's fine."

"Maybe she purges after," says McKenzie.

Can I die now? All I wanted to do was save money, and suddenly, I've been accused of having an eating disorder. And the worst, most shameful part? That's actually a little better than admitting I'm poor.

"Come on, you have to eat." Noah wheels me around to face the cashier. "Whatever she wants," he says, "it's on me." He smiles my way. "See? Now it would be rude to refuse to eat."

"But I don't need you to pay—" I dig into my pocket, trying not to hyperventilate at the cost.

"I owe you. I ate your lunch yesterday."

And with that, Noah saves me, and I fall into official friend-like with him. We're halfway through eating when Emily chokes down a mouthful of fries and says, "My phone!" She rises, slapping the pockets of her jeans.

"Check your bag," says Noah.

"It's not there," she says. "I always have it in my back pocket." She slides her hands along her hips and gives us a cheeky smile. "Although it's kind of easy to lose stuff in these curves."

"You sure have a lot of those," says McKenzie.

I glare at her before she can open her dump truck mouth any bigger and say something hurtful.

She turns red and shovels a forkful of butter chicken.

Amazing. She has enough sensitivity to know when she's being an almost-idiot about someone's weight, but not enough brains to recognize racial stupidity. At least Emily's feelings weren't hurt, and that counts for something.

"I should check the stores," says Emily. "Maybe it's still at a cash register or something."

"I'll go with you." McKenzie stands.

For a minute, I'm not sure if she's doing it by way of apology or if she's setting me up for sabotage. My heart's racing and my palms are sweating. Emily's the only friend I have. But then I take a breath and remind myself, it's Emily. She'd never bail on me for McKenzie.

The two of them take off, and I'm left with Noah. I shove food in my mouth and try to think of something intelligent to say, something that will make him be my friend, rather than just be nice to me.

"Nira." The shadow of Farah falls on me at the same time her voice reaches my ears. "What are you doing here?"

I'm offended at her tone, like I don't belong at the mall with all the other cool kids. But I don't say what I'm thinking, I go with a casual, "Hey," and spot the Farahbots watching and commentating at a distance.

But she's not looking at me. She's all about Noah. "Farah." She slides in next to him and jerks a thumb in my direction. "Her cousin."

"Noah," he replies, and winks at me. "Her friend."

Holy Christmas, my heart just stopped. Did he call me his friend? If I'm shocked, then the look on Farah's face is full-on blindsided. I cover my surprise with a mouthful of food. It also disguises the smug smile of satisfaction.

"What were you guys talking about?" She reaches in and takes a fry from Noah's plate.

I hate her for her confidence. It would never occur to her that people don't want her fingers in their food.

Noah's gaze flicks my way, and he must get how much I don't like or trust her because he says, "Nira's helping me with math."

Farah rolls her eyes. "It's always about homework with her." When he looks her way, she gives him a cover girl smile and flips her hair back with practiced ease.

If I tried that, I'd need a chiropractor and a heating pad.

"Not always," Noah says. "There's also the matter of the band audition."

I have no idea if he's defending me or tossing me to the Farah wolf.

Her eyes go wide, and she whips around to stare at me. "You're going to try out?"

I nod.

"And your parents are okay with that?"

Another nod. I cast a furtive glance at Noah, worried he's caught the tone in her voice. It's one thing for me to know how lunatic my parents can be about academics. I'd rather not broadcast it to the entire world.

She's still staring, but I can't place the emotion or understand the unspoken conversation.

"I'm looking forward to hearing her play," continues Noah. "Have you heard her?"

Farah shakes her head.

Noah's eyebrows go up, and he grins my way. "Wow, Super Spy. Does James Bond take lessons from you?"

My cousin almost chokes on the food in her mouth. "Super Spy? You gave her a nickname?"

It's taking everything in me not to punch her. Why does she have to ask it like I'm usually kept in the basement away from the elderly, children, and anyone else who might be traumatized by the sight and sound of me?

Her friends run up—the same ones from dinner that night—a gang of brown dolls, all dressed in tight jeans and sparkly jewelry. They hover around Farah, giggling at Noah. They make sure to ignore me. Farah, their queen, rises after a horrendous few minutes of flirting with Noah. She commands them away.

"Man, she's something," he says when they're out of range.

I watch them walk away. Their power is in the sway of their hips, the shift in their shoulders. Farah looks back, watches me for a minute.

I can't tell what she's thinking, but I can guess, and I don't like it. "Yeah." She breaks the staring contest, and my focus goes back to Noah. "That's one way to describe her."

He opens his mouth like he's going to ask me something. Then he changes his mind, shrugs, and smiles.

I want to ask him what he was going to say, but I'm too afraid

I already know. Farah's gorgeous. He probably wanted her number. I'm sick with relief that he didn't ask. No matter what he said to her, he and I are barely friends. The idea of losing him to Farah is too heavy a weight.

Emily and McKenzie get back a few minutes later, and Emily's face is flushed and pink. The sick feeling returns; the ground is shifting; the shadows are looming. The storm is heading my way.

CHAPTER SIX

FRICTION HAS
AN ELECTRIC CHARGE

The next few days are a mix of joy and pain. No one from the mall phones me for an interview, but McKenzie, Noah, and Emily get calls. And jobs. I blame my not getting a call on my clothes and hair. They told the store staff lies about me. But there's nothing I can do. What a punch line. I can't get a job because I don't have clothing that can impress, but I can't afford clothing to impress until I get a job. I'd talk to Grandma about it, but she's managed to convince Uncle Raj to let her visit for the week, so I'm on my own.

The bright side is that Emily's still my friend . . . I think. Noah and McKenzie cling to us like Siamese twins. Maybe Emily's still saving me a seat at the lunch table because McKenzie is there, but Emily wants me to sit by her. Maybe she doesn't care who sits at our table as long as I'm there. Still, something seismic is happening, and I don't know if it'll mean the end of my time with Emily. I want to know, but I'm too afraid to ask the questions.

Instead, I tell my troubles to Georgia. I spend most of my nights with him, playing scales and practicing everything from ZZ Top's "Legs" to Bach's Gavotte No. 2 in F Major. I don't know what kind of music I'll be asked to play, and I want to be prepared for anything the teacher asks. Noah told me there's also a sight-reading part to the audition. Mr. Nam will give me a sheet of music, give me two minutes to look it over, and then I'll have to play it for him.

Georgia doesn't mind the extra hours of practice, and I'm enjoying all the time we have together. Since it's now considered school related, Mom and Dad aren't giving me the gears about how much time I'm playing. There's something about having their permission that's opened space inside of me. It's like my lungs are three times bigger than they used to be, and there's a texture of emotion, range, and volume I've gained.

It's so weird, how things can be so great but so uncertain at the same time. The best and worst is my time with Noah. He's funny and most of all, he's kind. He's the kindest person I've ever known. If I had fifty fewer IQ points, I would probably fall for him, but I'm smart enough to only reach for what I can grasp.

Still, I feel like I'm living on a fault line. Everything's great, but I feel like there's rumbling deep down where I can't see or feel it, and something's going to blow. Mom and Dad will change their mind. I won't get a spot in jazz band. Noah will turn out to be a jerk. McKenzie will take my spot as Emily's best friend. Emily will realize what a loser I am.

I try to keep the anxiety quiet as I sit by Emily at lunch and talk about my job woes. Noah's gone—his dad's taken him on another adventure. McKenzie, mercifully, is at a dentist appointment, which means I get Emily to myself. I didn't realize how much I missed my alone time with her until I didn't have it anymore.

"My mom and I were at the mall last weekend. Junta is hiring," she says.

Junta. I walked in once, looked at the prices, and walked out. But if I worked there, if I belonged, it would be different. I imagine myself under the recessed lights, surrounded by dark wood, clothing stacked into precise lines, the smell of pineapples in the air.

"You get a discount if you work there."

My brain goes dreamy at the thought of walking down the street in clothes that proclaim my worth. "If I get the job—"

"When," Emily corrects me. "They'd be nuts not to hire you."

"—I'll share my discount."

She bumps my shoulder. "That's mighty kind of you—" She waves and I turn in the direction.

McKenzie.

"Didn't she have a dentist appointment?"

"Just to change out her inlines," says Emily. "That doesn't take too long."

"We should do something, just the two of us. We haven't had enough of that."

Emily nods. Then she grins. "She drives you crazy, doesn't she?"

"McKenzie? Uh—" I have to tread carefully. Emily likes her. Then again, Emily's the kind of person who sees the best in people, even if she has to turn her head and squint. I want to trust our friendship, but I blurt out, "Don't you find her . . . stupid?"

Emily laughs. "Not everyone has brains like you." She takes a sip of her pop. "McKenzie has a different kind of intelligence, and in her way, she's smart. She's funny, too."

There's a warning in her words, but I try again to push my toe across the line. "But her jokes always seem to make me the punch line."

"That's not true." Emily squeezes my hand. "I think you feel it because you don't like her. You see the worst in her. Maybe if you looked for the things that you have in common, you'd see she's cool."

The only thing we have in common is Emily, and she's just told me everything I need to know. On the one hand, it makes me love her more. Emily has a knack for bringing out the best in people.

Me, on the other hand, not so much. For sure, McKenzie and I bring out the worst in each other. I only have one option. Keep my mouth shut. Emily likes McKenzie, which means our duo is now a trio. All I can do is hope I learn how to stand McKenzie—or at least learn how to keep my contempt from showing. Who knows, maybe the gods will smile on me and I'll see in McKenzie what Emily does. I doubt it. The gods have never smiled on me.

McKenzie slides in next to Emily and helps herself to my friend's food. "Do you feel ready?"

I have no idea what she's talking about.

"The audition," Emily translates.

"Oh, yeah. I guess. I mean, I still have a couple of days."

"Weeks," says McKenzie. "The auditions got pushed back." She squints like I'm an interesting specimen she's found under the microscope. "Didn't you get the e-mail?"

I shake my head.

She pulls out her phone and calls up the message. I take the cell and read. Auditions have been pushed back. Mr. Nam's wife had to be induced; the baby's in the Natal Intensive Care Unit. He's listed the times he's available for—"Instrument inspection"?

"Did you take your trumpet to Mr. Nam?" asks McKenzie.

"No, I didn't get the e-mail."

Another squint. "You're sure you didn't get the message?"

"Why would I lie about it?"

Emily takes McKenzie's phone and looks. "In the group mail, he added an 'e' to your last name."

"I'll have to e-mail him and correct it." I'm trying to remember the schedule Mr. Nam set for the inspection. Do I have time to get a real trumpet? The thought of bringing Georgia to school and being laughed at is making my hands shake.

McKenzie takes the phone back. "It's weird how the cutbacks worked out in everyone's favor. You know your instrument better than anything the school might let you rent."

Rent. I can rent a real trumpet from Reynolds. If my memory's right, then I have time to pick it up before the inspection. The shaky feeling disappears, and the food in my stomach stops dancing. Renting an instrument means a monthly cost. Which means I'll blow my allowance on one thing.

The gastrointestinal rumba picks up again. Now, more than ever, I have to get a job, and I don't have time to learn all the instruments and accessories at Reynolds. It'll have to be a position at the mall. After school, I'll print off more résumés and then take them around. I have less than two weeks to get work, but one way or another, I'm going to make it happen.

———◦———

Junta is the last place I drop off my résumé—I need the time to screw up my courage. The manager is there and says, "It's quiet. Why don't we talk now?"

I'm not dressed for an interview and I'm not in the correct

mental space, but I say, "Sure." When she's not looking, I wipe the dampness from my hands on my jeans. We go to a set of red leather couches that sits in front of a fast-food burger kiosk. I wait while she looks over my information. I check my teeth with my tongue to make sure there's nothing hidden or stuck between them.

"Bibi?" Her gaze lifts.

"Yes." I stick my hand out.

She shakes, and I can tell by the look in her eye that I've scored a point.

"I go by Nira."

"Hmm." The tip of her pen slips between her lips as she scans the pages again. "Bibi is easier for people to read and pronounce than Nira." She smiles my way.

I don't think that's true, but I'm pretty sure this is a test. So I smile back. "That's fine. I'm happy to go with Bibi if that's easier for the clientele."

"We like to think of them as friends. We push a fun, bestie, intimate atmosphere. Here at Junta, we're not just engaging in a consumer interaction; we're about the experience. It's about connection, seeing each other as individuals but also seeing the commonality, the essence we share as fellow human beings."

That's a lot of pressure for two meters of cotton and several yards of thread, but okay.

"Junta's about changing the world through our brand, one

shirt at a time. When you see someone wearing Junta, you know they're just like you."

Okay, now I'm worried about (1) why I'm so hung up on clothes, and (2) whether I'm applying for a job or joining some kind of cotton religion. But I remind myself there's a trumpet at stake. "Of course. I apologize for calling them clients."

The interview continues. Some of the answers I know: "I can work Friday afternoons, all day Saturday, and Sunday afternoon." She pushes for more hours, but I tell her I can't because of my studies. That sounds better than "I can't. My mom and dad won't let me." Just so she doesn't write me off, I give her the best spiel I can about my desire for world change and how I believe a combination of education, work, and the right clothes from Junta can bring us world peace.

Some of the answers are harder to find, like when she asks what I can offer as an employee that others can't. Pledging my undying devotion and eternal loyalty seems needy, so I say, "I take my job seriously and will endeavor to make sure I am the best representation of your brand." I want to add, "Plus, I'm colored, so there's diversity." But I've seen the models on their walls and in their magazine. Diversity for them stops with redheads.

"Tell me about some of your favorite fashion looks."

Favorite fashion looks? Great. Another job I should have studied for. "My look is casual"—I ignore the three lines that form in her forehead and plunge ahead—"fun sweaters, worn jeans." I'm describing one of the billboards, but I don't want to be obvious about it. "I like outfits that do double duty. A pair of faded jeans, button-up white shirt. Pair it with sandals for a relaxed look or add heels and some sparkle for a night out." I say it all like I'm not wearing old jeans and a beat-up hoodie.

She nods.

I hold my breath and hope I've nailed it.

She looks at my clothes and my inner glow dims. "We do require our family members to wear our brand."

I'm starting to feel like I'm signing up for a cult. New vocabulary—not customers, friends. Not employees, family. And we have to dress the same. Plus, there's the whole affecting global change with our smile. "That's not a problem."

"Which of our clothing line do you have now?"

I'm sure she can see the rising red of embarrassment through my dark skin.

"If you want to update your look, you're welcome to shop beforehand. Some stores will put it on your account, then take it out of your first paycheck, but we don't operate like that. However, you'll get a thirty-five percent discount."

I can't wait to go home and tell my parents that I got a job and I'll have my own money, and, uh, could they please front me a couple hundred dollars to update my wardrobe.

My thoughts must show on my face.

"We're looking for members who will add to our collective, not kids looking to expand their wardrobe at our expense."

She didn't understand my look. "That's not what I was thinking."

"Then what was it?"

I want to tell her that, for my family, a couple hundred dollars is a king's ransom, that it's food for a week, and not everyone's born into a family where buying jeans and shirts is a nothing event, and maybe her "family" should wake up and understand that. But I don't. I can't. I just mumble, "Thanks for your time," and leave.

When I get home, Mom asks, "How did it go?"

"Like everything else, I guess." I go to my room and cry. When the tears are done, I take my sorrows to Georgia. Together, we play "Almost Blue." He tells me he understands my pain in the round tone of his bell and the smooth slide of the valves against my fingertips. I return the love with every breath, with every pause between the notes. We don't get a lot of time together because we have to go to Farah's house for dinner. Grandma calls my name, and I clean up Georgia and set him down in the blue velvet-lined case.

When we get to the house, I see no other shoes by the door. Thank god, it's just them and us. After my day, I can't handle any Farahbots. My cousin's waiting for me at the foot of the stairs. As soon as I put away my coat, she takes me to her room.

I follow her up the stairs, and have one of those moments when

I wish they would come to our place, so I didn't have to be surrounded by all her stuff. Then I think about our yellow bathroom with the seventies taps, the fake wood panel of my bedroom wall, the neon sunflower paper in the kitchen, and I'm happy they rarely see the inside of our house. Anyway, with the way my uncle drinks, it's probably a good thing to keep him contained within his walls instead of out on the road.

"What's going on with you and Noah?" She takes a drag of her cigarette and exhales the smoke through the open window.

"We're friends."

"Just friends?"

I can't hide my irritation. "Why? Do you want him or something?"

"Or something," she speaks more to the night air than me.

"What does that mean?" I perch on the edge of her bed, too intimidated to put a dent in the perfect fluff of her down duvet.

"I saw you with those other girls, too, in the mall. The two blondes."

"So, what are you? The people police?"

"What do you even talk about?" She takes another drag.

"I don't know." My irritation's growing. "The same things as you and your friends, I guess."

She gives me that smile—the one I always want to punch off her face. "I doubt it."

I stand. "I should see if Mom or Aunty Gul need help with dinner or setting the table."

"Nira." The smile hasn't left her face. "Always so good."

I leave her to her cancer stick and go downstairs. Grandma is setting the table.

"I thought you were with Farah."

"I did my penance." I take the dishes from her and shoo her to a chair.

She sits with a tired sigh. "Nira, such a good girl."

When she says it, it doesn't sound like a taunt.

"Did you and Farah fight?"

The question is a version of the coded message she asks every time we come here. Why can't you and Farah get along? I can never bring myself to tell Grandma the truth of Farah. "Are you okay?"

"The price of getting old. Your joints hurt and your bones tell you if it's going to rain."

"I'll finish setting the table." It's a sacrifice because that means going into the heart of the kitchen with Aunty Gul and Mom. When I get there, they're too busy arguing over the consistency of the cassava pone to pay attention to me.

Fifteen minutes later, everyone's sitting down to dinner.

"So, Nira." Uncle Raj unfolds his white napkin and sets it in his lap. "How is school going for you?"

"Good." I break off a piece of sada roti.

"Didn't you have a chemistry test?"

Amazing. The man can't remember my birthday, but he remembers my school curriculum better than I do. "Yeah, it was fine."

"What was your mark?"

Dad pauses. He's just remembered about the test. The look on his face is part panic, part exasperation. Raj is younger than him, and their sibling rivalry trickles down to their children. It's not just my honor on the line. It's his, too.

"A-minus."

My uncle's eyes go wide. "A-minus?"

I nod.

He smirks. "Where did the missing points go? Did they fall off your desk?"

"I did my best," I tell him.

"Did your best." His lips twist as he mimics me. "How Canadian of you. But you're not Canadian, Nira. You're Guyanese, and your parents didn't bring you here to do your best. They brought you here to do better than your best."

Farah's eyes glaze over. She's heard this rant before.

"It's physically impossible to do better than my best," I say. "Best is a binary function. It either is or isn't."

The smirk freezes on his mouth. He knows I'm insolent, but since I'm not belligerent, he can't do anything. Until Noah and

McKenzie came into my life, I'd never have dared talk to him like this. But there must be something in numbers, in having a pack—even if you're not a hundred percent sure they're your pack—that makes a person bold.

Dad's expression warns me I'm treading close to the wrong side of the line. I can't risk him getting mad enough to ground me or take away the job or the audition.

I smile. "Next time I'll do better. After all, I'm a Ghani, right? We're born to be the best." Then to make sure I'm out of the danger zone, I nod in Farah's direction and add, "Even if I'm always chasing that one."

Dad relaxes, and Uncle Raj is back to full smirk. The world is turning as it should.

"Can Nira come with us to Cape Canaveral?" Farah asks, and the earth screeches to a stop.

"What?" I stammer. Mom's glaring at me. So is Dad. There's no way to tell them I didn't approve of her request.

Mom's laugh is high and forced. "Nira, the pot salt, always has to be in the mix."

"That's not fair," I say. "I'm not a pot salt." In this scenario, I'm more like the lobster trying to escape the pot.

"There are four tickets," says Farah. "Nira and I were talking about it—"

God, I'm going to suffer third-degree burns from my parents' glares. "I only told her congratulations." I hold up my hands in surrender.

I know how the politics of our two families work. We're not the share and share alike household. We may eat dinner together once a week, but it's not out of familial piety. It's to compare scores and see who won the game of life for the week. Which kid got the higher mark? Whose wife got the better deal at the store? We don't go on vacation together, and for sure, there's no sharing of bounty.

Uncle Raj weighs the con of having me tag along. Then again, his eyes seem to say, I've got my older brother's daughter in a five-star hotel with a five-star pool and food. And I can lord that over him for years. The decision is made in the blink of his eye.

"It's an extra ticket," he says. "It would be a shame to waste it."

"Maybe you should take one of your friends," I tell Farah. Or anyone who won't try to smother you in your sleep.

"No," says Aunty Gul, picking up on the opportunity to shove their wealth in our faces. "It should be family."

"Take Grandma," I say, and the old lady shoots me a look of panic. Oops. I figured since it was her son, she wouldn't care, but it's obvious she finds him as insufferable as the rest of us.

"It would be a great opportunity for Nira." My uncle spreads his hands. "She'll be able to take the tour of NASA with Farah and talk to the scientists."

Ugh. That's a genius play. Mom and Dad go quiet. A life of

listening to Raj and Gul gloat about how they spoiled me at their own expense, versus the chance for me to expand my learning and talk to actual astronauts. They don't have to blink for me to know what their decision will be. They sacrificed good jobs, money, and a big house so I could have a better life in Canada. What's a bit of their pride?

"When is the trip?" I ask.

"Why?" Uncle Raj tips the sides of his mouth. "Big test coming up? You need extra time to study and make up for your terrible marks?"

"I have an audition in a few weeks—"

"Audition?" Aunty Gul turns to Mom. "You didn't say anything about that."

"It's for band," I blurt out, then catch my dad's pressed mouth and squinting eyes—his trademark signal for shut up.

Uncle Raj chokes on his rum. "Band? Band? You're letting her play in band?"

"It's good for her university application," says Dad. "More rounded."

He snorts. "Big whoop. Band. It's not a trip to Florida to meet the people who make the space shuttle." Uncle Raj smiles at me. "You'll come, *betee.*"

I grit my teeth at him calling me daughter. "I can't. I've signed up."

"Nira," says Dad. "Your uncle and aunty are being very generous."

It's tempting to point out that passing on a ticket they didn't pay for is recycling, not generosity, but I keep my mouth closed. "I know, and I appreciate it, but I'm on the list."

"Big deal," presses Uncle Raj. "It's not like you're the only one who plays—whatever you play—at school. Besides, you're not even formally trained. Do you think you'll get a spot?"

The subtext of his words splinters us into a strained silence. Your family can't afford to pay for lessons. You're too stupid to teach yourself. No one will want you.

"I have the brains my parents gave me," I tell him. "I know how to search out tutorials on the Internet, and I know how to play by ear."

"She's a true musician." Grandma takes my hand. "A skinny Louis Armstrong."

Uncle Raj is smiling at her. He looks like a kid whose had his hand slapped, knows he deserves it, but isn't willing to back down. "I'm sure she's good. But NASA—"

"The trip won't mess with the audition," Farah says. "You can come."

"Band," sneers Uncle Raj. "Listen to me—"

"How was your day, Farah?" Grandma talks over him like he's not even there. The matriarch has spoken, and we all fall in line with Grandma's hint to change the subject. But even as the conversation turns from soccer to politics and the coming winter, my uncle's words and his attempt to embarrass my parents casts its shadow over us. All I can do is hope to leave it behind when the night finishes.

———◇———

"Nira." Dad knocks on my door and steps inside. "I want to talk to you about tonight."

"I'm not going on that stupid trip."

He raises his hand, placating. "Your aunty and uncle are difficult to deal with, but this opportunity—"

"Opportunity? Opportunity? For what? To have them buy Farah a bunch of clothes and souvenirs and I get to watch?"

He sits on my bed. "I'm sure they would buy you things as well—"

"Won't that be great?" The bitterness is on my tongue and in my words. "They can talk about it every time I see them."

"Your mother and I can give you money."

"I don't want money." I fold my arms across my chest, part defiance, part protective. "I don't want to go."

"Put your pride in your pocket for a minute," he says. "Think of what you can learn—"

"I'm always learning! My whole stupid life is learning! For

once, just once in my loser life—"

"Don't say that! You're not a loser, and this life isn't stupid."

"Maybe not." I'm rubbing my arms to keep myself from crying. "But this isn't my life."

He mutters to himself and rolls his eyes. "Not again. This is an opportunity." He holds up his hand when I try to talk. "You won't be able to do any of these things when you're older. You'll have work and the expense of travel. Now is the time to learn as much as you can."

"You told me I could try out for jazz band."

"That will come again next year when you're a senior. This is a once-in-a-lifetime chance."

No amount of arm rubbing can stop the tears pricking my eyes. "You said I could."

"Nira." His tone is exasperated but loving. "Do you know what I would have done for a chance like this?"

"Probably the same thing I would do for a chance at jazz band."

His mouth thins into a flat line. "I won't tell you what to do—" He stops talking as Grandma comes into the room, carrying two cups of tea. She sets mine down on the desk and takes the second cup to Dad.

"You're called to do big things. If you want to waste your time blowing on a piece of tin, fine. But your life will pass you by, and you will look back on this with regret."

"I won't ever regret doing the things that make me happy."

"I want to stay home and watch cricket all day." He balances the cup on his lap, then shifts it to his knees when the heat burns him. "That will make me happy, but it will also make me homeless. You must learn now to sacrifice—"

"I have sacrificed!" I hear the shrillness in my voice and tone it down. "I don't go to parties or sleepovers. I'm not on any teams— all I do is study. Why do I have to fight you on this one thing I want, when I do everything you ask me?"

He shoots me an impatient look that asks how can I be so monumentally stupid. "All this talk of happiness. No discussion of responsibility. That's—"

"How kids end up in the gutter," I finish.

"Don't get fresh with me. It's true."

"Yeah?" The challenge is in the lift of my eyebrows. "You see a lot of kids in the gutters?"

"Maybe not here, but back home, yes. You think the white bank managers want to hire a brown kid when they can hire a white one? You had to be smarter and work harder—"

"Back then skin color mattered. But now it doesn't matter like it did before." I take a deep breath. "I deserve this, Dad. I'm a good kid with good marks, and I don't cause you trouble."

He snorts.

"I'm a good kid." My mouth is dry, but I'm pushing. I want my parents to be happy and proud of me, but I need this. "All I want is a sliver," I tell my dad. "Just a piece of this world that can be mine."

I see the connection on his face, and for a minute, I think I've won.

He frowns. "You're not like anyone else and being different always matters. The only way you fight it is with hard work and education."

Grandma and I exchange a glance. She sits in the chair by the desk and watches, ready to step in, but this fight is mine.

"It's not about being different," I say to him. "It's about being myself. I want to play in jazz band—"

"Nira—"

"Life's also about having character and keeping your word." I'm sweating through my clothes, but I refuse to back down. "Did your word not mean anything? Did you lie to me?"

He scowls. "No, but—"

"Sometimes I'm going to say no to one thing because I've said yes to something else." My voice is a dim drone, drowned out by the thumping of my heart. "I committed to the audition. If the trip doesn't conflict, I'll go, but this is my priority."

He glares at me, and it takes all my strength to maintain eye contact. After a minute, Dad sighs and leaves the room.

I lift the cup of tea with shaking hands and take a sip. Hot, with just the right amount of sugar and milk.

Grandma puts her hand on my shoulder. "I knew you could win this fight. You and me, girl, we're cut from the same cloth. Play me some Irving Berlin. Later, come for a walk with me."

I nod, and she leaves. I get Georgia and hold him close; I take a breath, and the opening of "What'll I Do?" fills the space and my heart. Another breath and I blow, hoping the tune fills my grandmother's heart as well.

As soon as the weekend hits, I head to Reynolds.

"I talked to Masao," Alec says. "It's sorted. You can work here."

"But I don't know anything about"—I wave my hand around the room—"any of it."

"You know music, right? You know what a trombone is and what a violin is—"

"Yeah, but you said Masao wants experts."

"You will be." He smiles. "He's gone for a while, so I have time to teach you everything."

"But—"

"Nira, trust me, you'll be golden. I knew it from the first time we talked. You belong here."

Why am I fighting this? Why am I arguing when it's exactly what I want? I push down the insecurity and let the happiness take flight. "Okay, I'm in."

I fill out the paperwork and get a name tag. Then we spend the morning with him showing me how to work the cash register, what the guitar picks look like, the difference in violin bows. It's like trying to shower under a waterfall—too much of everything and too powerful, and it's all going to drown me—but what a way to go.

As I'm leaving, I ask about the employee discount and about buying a new trumpet. He gives me a wicked discount on a Bach TR200S. Alec tells me I can rent it and he'll take it out of my first paycheck. I e-mail Mr. Nam to set up an inspection time for the trumpet, then head home.

———◇———

"You should come with me," says Emily when I tell her about what happened at Junta, and how much I hate not having money to buy stuff.

I wait for her to fill in the blanks, then sigh and wave my hand in a circle when I realize she's doing her psychic twin thing. "I'm too upset to read your mind."

"You should come to the consignment shop with me."

"Consignment?"

"You know, used."

"I'm not sure buying secondhand will be better than bargain basement stuff."

"It's not that kind of place. It's high-end stuff." She takes a bite of her hoagie. "Most of it is suburban mom stuff. You know, wealthy ladies who're going through a divorce and are selling off their designer stuff until the alimony comes through. Mom took me to it when she was divorcing Roger." She pauses in midchew. "Maybe it was Bill. No, wait. Michael. It was Michael."

"What are the prices like?"

"Joel! It was Joel." She splays her hands and starts counting on her fingers. "Hold on. Roger, Bill—"

I cover her fingers and ask my question again.

"The prices are excellent. Better than discount and the shop owner is psycho about making sure everything looks brand-new. You can't tell the clothes are used. Some of them still have price tags." She smiles and goes back to eating.

It takes two days of negotiating with Mom and Dad, but I get permission to go shopping with Emily after school.

"This is a big deal," says my mom. "I expect your marks to stay the same."

"One day of hanging out after school won't drop my grades."

"It's not one day." Dad's voice sounds from behind the newspaper. "It's how one day rolls into two then three. Soon, you're skipping school. That's how kids end up in the gutter."

"But think how good I'll look with my new clothes."

The paper flips down with a crinkle, and he stares me down.

I toss a grin his way.

"What is this place called?" The paper covers his face once more.

"No idea."

"Weird name."

Everyone's a comedian. "That's not the name. I don't know the name. She just said she'd take me shopping."

He sets down his paper. "Did you hear what your daughter said?"

Mom and I exchange a confused glance. Bad things happen when he talks about me like he's not responsible for fifty percent of my DNA.

"She's going off with some girl we don't know—"

"Raul, the girl sleeps over! You know her!"

"—and she's going to someplace where she doesn't know the name."

"Before you tell me how this will end me up in a gutter, it's safe. Emily and her mom go there all the time."

"Serial killers love unprotected girls who adhere to a routine," says Dad.

"I'm a brown girl in a city full of white people. Statistically speaking, the murderer is most likely to be white, and serial killers tend to prefer victims of their color."

His eyes go wide. "What have you been reading?"

"Everything since you won't spring for premium cable or Internet."

"Books are better than TV, anyway," he grunts. "Uplift your mind."

"Tell that to Lady Chatterley."

"Eh?"

"Nothing. Thanks for letting me go."

"I expect you to be responsible about your purchases," he says. "None of these shorty shorts with half your cheesecake hanging out."

I'm not sure what body part the cheesecake is, but I nod. "No showing the desserts."

"And remember, just because you have the money doesn't mean you have to spend it."

"Right."

"It's not like it's burning a hole in your pocket."

"Right."

"You can think about the clothes and go back."

I shoot a look at Mom. Is this going to end, or is he going to keep talking until I decide to repurpose the rice bags and use the money for a registered education saving plan? I dash for escape before he can change his mind.

"Make sure your homework's done," is his final parting shot.

———◇———

The Nu4U store might end up being my new favorite place. Emily was right on about the prices and the clothes. I figured I'd only get a couple of things because I don't have loads to spend, but I get tons of stuff.

I blow my budget but get two fabulous interview outfits—black skirt, cardi, and white button-down, a pair of skinny crepe pants and a printed peasant blouse. I love them because they'll do double duty for casual school outfits, but I also love them because they're high quality. The kind of brand name that doesn't need a logo sprayed on the front. Plus, I got other stuff—jeans, leggings, shirts. I can't wait to walk into school. I'm flying high as I head home, glide through the door, and head into the kitchen

Mom turns from the stove and smiles at the bags. "Success. Did you leave anything in the store?"

"A saleslady with the happy afterglow of having earned her minimum wage."

"Let me make tea, and then you give us a show."

Grandma is already up from the table, setting out the cups and milk.

Dad comes in, eyes me up and down. "Is anything left in your bank account?"

"Yes—"

"How much?"

"It'll carry me to my next paycheck"

"All your money, on clothes? Nothing saved, you wasted it all—"

"But it's not a waste." I set down the bags. "The saleslady said the pieces are classic, so later I can use them at college interviews."

His expression of disgust is so exquisite, Google maps could GPS every pore on his skin. "You're so naive. It's her job. Nira, I trusted you to be responsible—"

"I am responsible! Look at all the stuff I got for the money."

"Cheap clothes that will fall apart in the wash. You could've gotten a microscope with the money. I can't believe you wasted money like this."

Why can't I ever win with him? "For what? To study the soap scum on the bathroom tile? Wanting fun stuff isn't a bad thing!"

"I told you to save some of your money."

"It's my money!"

"That we give you!"

"That I earn! God, this is why I wanted a job of my own. Then you can't tell me how to spend my money!"

He takes one of the bags from my grasp and dumps it on the table.

What is his damage?

He picks up the clothing, one at a time, then drops them like they're dirty cleaning rags.

It's taking everything in me not to yell and scream.

"They don't even have proper tags. What happens if you change your mind?"

"I won't change my mind, and even if I did, there are no refunds."

His eyes go raging bull-wide, and he spins to face Mom. "You let your daughter do this?"

"Do what, Raul? It's fun for her, and she needs to enjoy—"

"For this? What kind of place doesn't have refunds?"

"It's a consignment shop." I grab the clothes from him and stuff them in the bag.

Three horizontal lines form on his forehead. "What's consignment?"

"People sell their clothes."

He's giving me a blank look. "Isn't that a regular store?"

"No, it's—reselling."

The blood drains from his face so completely that he turns a chalky shade of white. "Resell?" He whispers the word. "This is used? You bought other people's garbage?"

"It's not garbage—"

"The garbage they don't want! Things they would dump, you buy it!"

I'm going to give myself whiplash, trying to look at Mom,

Grandma, and Dad, trying to look at them all at once.

He's yelling, but the weird kind of screaming parents do. The kind when they're so angry, they can't even turn up the volume because their vocal cords are tight with rage. And I can't catch what he's saying. He's switched to Guyanese Creole, and I'm rusty with the language.

"Dad, Dad, talk to me. I don't understand."

"How could you do this, Nira? How could you take everything we've done for you and throw it away?"

"On clothes?" I'm not angry anymore. I'm too scared and confused. Mom and Grandma aren't any help. Mom's staring, as worried and frightened as I am. Grandma's expression I can't read, and I don't have time to figure it out because Dad's consuming my attention.

"Do you know what we sacrificed to get here?"

"What? Dad—" I can't get the rest of the words out because the tears clog my throat. I've never seen him like this, and I don't know what to do.

"We may be poor." He stabs the clothes. "But we will never be this poor."

"This isn't about poor—lots of kids—"

But he's not listening, he's not even here in the kitchen, anymore. He's in some other world where no one can reach him. Dad hefts the bags off the table and storms for the back door.

"What are you doing?" I chase after him and try to free one of the bags.

"We will never wear other people's castoffs!"

He bursts through the door, the bags swinging at his side. He wrenches open the garbage lid.

Horror stops me midstride. "What are you doing?" I blink, and suddenly my clothes are falling through plastic and into discarded banana peels, rotting meat, and used tissues.

"What are you doing? What are you doing?" I run to the garbage, but he's tying the bag and hefting it out. "That's my stuff! You can't do that to my stuff!"

"It's not yours, it's someone else's, and this is where it belongs." He pushes past me.

"What is wrong with you? That was mine!"

"As long as you're under my care, it's all my stuff."

"Are you going to pay me back for the money I spent?" I yell at his retreating figure.

But he's out the yard and heading to the garage. Mom chases after him. Grandma comes out of the house. Blurred vision and salty tears takes me to the tree stump.

"It's my fault." Grandma presses the cup into my hand.

"I doubt it."

"We were so poor, so poor, anything we got was because of other people. Clothes, food. Sometimes even water." She wipes the tears from my face. "There are two kinds of people in the world, Nira. The people who will give to you because your heart and theirs beat together." She takes my hand. "But then there are those who give to you, not because they want to hold their hand out to you, but because they want to hold their hand over you. To remind you of their generosity every time they see you. To remind you that you would be nothing without them."

"I'm sorry, Grandma, but—"

"Your dad grew up hearing those words in his ears. That he was nothing without these people to put clothes on his back. It was humiliating. Degrading. He told me once he would rather have gone naked than have to hear one more child tell him about his used clothes." She points to the cup. "Drink."

"I'm not thirsty."

"Drink."

I drink. The tea is hot and sweet and creamy, but it can't take the bitter taste from my mouth, and it can't stop the icy cold that's spreading inside me. I want to wail and howl, but I'm afraid if I start, I'll never stop.

"It's hard to let go of those things. He's afraid for you."

"No, he isn't. He's thinking about having to explain to Uncle Raj and Aunty Gul that his daughter bought secondhand."

She winces. "Okay, maybe that, too, but try to understand."

I shake my head. "I always have to do that. Understand the

life inside these walls isn't the same as the life outside these walls. Why can't he be the one who understands, for once?"

"I'll talk to him."

"No, don't." I drain the last of my tea and press my warm hands up to my forehead, hoping to relieve the tight muscles. "I'm tired of talking to them and begging for everything. I hate my life. Do you think white kids have to do the same thing with their parents?"

She pats my lap. "Every kid has to wrestle with their parents."

Maybe, but I doubt Noah or McKenzie have to deal with anything like this. We head inside, and I go to my room. I take out my phone and text Emily, but I don't get a reply. She's probably out with her mom or she's misplaced her phone. I reach for the new trumpet, but habit makes me take Georgia. I'm okay with that. At times like these, I'd rather have an old friend to comfort me.

———◇———

I've just finished the last note from Louis Armstrong's "Hello, Dolly!" when I hear the front door open and my parents' voices in the hallway. It's too soon for them to return. I want to play the song again, to feel my lungs burn and strain at the high notes, to weary my fingers on the keys. But to play is to shout my presence in the house. Even though they know I'm home, I don't want to be in their minds or awareness. I want to be left alone. I blow the spit from the valve and put Georgia on the bed beside me.

There's a knock at my door, Dad asking to come in.

I stay quiet.

He knocks again. And again.

He gets nothing from me.

There's another knock. Softer. "Please, Nira," says Grandma. "Open the door."

I do, then step into the hallway. "If I'm going to get yelled at again, I don't want to be yelled at in my room. Oh. Sorry. I mean your room that I get to live in because I decided to be born. No, wait, that was your decision. Just like moving us here. Just like throwing out my clothes."

I move to the kitchen table and challenge him with a look.

Grandma goes to the kettle.

"No," I tell her. "No tea. Not everything can be solved with tea."

"I'm thirsty," she replies, and adds with a lift of her mouth, "And you ain't my mother."

"I don't talk a lot about myself or how I grew up." Dad sits across from me. "That's not my style."

"If this is about the poverty you grew up in, Grandma already told me."

His eyes slide in her direction but come back to me. Dad clasps his hands and rests them between his knees. "You can't explain being poor. It's something you feel, and you experience. It gets in your bones and blood, and it changes your DNA. Your toilet is a bush. You save rainwater because it's all the water you get." His mouth softens as he looks at Grandma. "One tea bag for three people and it has to last the day." His attention returns to the table. "The poor we were, Nira, you can't understand."

I open my mouth to argue, but he's still talking.

"I'm sorry we're still poor, but money was the price we paid to move here. We don't have money for the clothes you want or the life you want, but we have money to put food on the table and for you to have a fresh cup of tea whenever you want."

His smile is a spear of guilt in my heart. I don't want to understand him or forgive him, but the images of the child-him are in my brain and shredding down my resentment.

"My clothes are gone. My money is gone. You talk about being poor and being responsible, but I spent the money, and now it's nowhere. How is that being good?"

The smile fades. "It's not. I acted badly."

That's as much of an "I'm sorry" as I'll ever get from him. "This place isn't like Guyana, okay? Wearing used clothes is . . ." I don't want to say cool. ". . . not an uncool thing." I get up. "It's okay to recycle and reuse. You talk about how hard it is for you guys. Do you ever think about what it's like for me? There's a world between these walls that doesn't exist once I walk out the door. Little Guyana smack in the middle of America." I can't say it right, can't make him see. But I don't want to stay in the kitchen anymore because the longer I look at him, the more he looks like a kid. The more he reminds me of me, poor and trying to fit in, railing against the life he didn't choose.

I go to my room and spend the rest of the night doing homework and practicing with Georgia. When I wake up, the clothes I bought are at the foot of the bed and folded in precise lines. My gaze goes around the room. The work clothes have been pressed and put on hangers on the closet knob. I lift a shirt to my nose and inhale. It smells of detergent and dryer sheets, but there's another scent.

My dad's cologne.

He took the clothes out of the garbage. He washed and dried them. He folded them. Maybe in other houses, that's nothing. In our family, my dad doing laundry is headline news. I stumble from my bed and run through the house, looking for him. He's at the sink, drinking his tea, and he turns when he hears me. I run into his arms, crying. Dad hugs me tight, and that's all the sorry I need.

CHAPTER SEVEN

RESENTMENT IS A TOXIC CLOUD

'm at work on Saturday night when Emily comes in for our night together.

"I wasn't sure if you'd realize we were waiting for you."

"We?"

"I thought it would be fun to bring Mac and Noah."

Is she kidding? Tonight was just supposed to be the two of us— and what's up with calling her Mac? "It was supposed to be you and me, not you, me, and everyone else."

"It's fine. They wanted to join in, and I don't see the problem." She turns as they come in.

I swallow the rising anxiety, but it won't stay down. The gap is growing between Emily and me, and I don't know how to stop it.

"So, you're hanging out with Emie and me, hey?" asks McKenzie.

I press my lips together and stay quiet. What's with her calling my friend Emie? Was there a nickname meeting and no one invited me?

"It's going to be so much fun," says Emily. "You should hear Mac's impressions. She's hilarious."

Quick, someone put a piece of coal between my lips, because I'm pressing them together so hard I could make a diamond.

"Ready to party?" asks Noah as he walks up.

"It's been a long day, and I'm not sure—"

"It's dinner and a movie," he says, "all you have to do is sit. Promise."

Hanging with Noah would be awesome. Hanging with McKenzie will be an exercise in torment. I hedge my indecision. "Yeah, that's what Emily and I had planned."

"I know." He grins. "My master plan to get you to say yes."

My skin flashes hot and cold. I don't know which topic to focus on, Emily suddenly calling my nemesis "Mac," or that Noah wants me to say yes to something.

"Did you get the e-mail from Mr. Nam?" asks McKenzie. "Or did you lose it again?"

"I never lost—" Why do I bother? I take out my phone and check. "No, nothing."

"The auditions are pushed back again," says Noah.

"Again!" God. Mr. Nam's cancelled my instrument inspection

twice. Plus, Dad's making rumblings. He wants to change his mind, and the only thing stopping him is knowing the audition is coming up. If I go and tell him it's been changed—again—I know what will happen. He'll twist it around and say that Mr. Nam is irresponsible, and then I'll never get to play.

Emily's face crumples. "Oh, no, because of his family?"

Noah nods, and I sink into the floor. Trust Emily to put it in perspective for me. Way to go, Nira. Lose your mind on your stuff. Meanwhile, the guy's worried about a wife and a near-death baby. "Is there anything we can do for him?"

"You're sweet." Noah throws his arm around my shoulder.

If only he knew the thoughts that go through my head. "You obviously don't know me as well as you think you do."

"And whose fault is that, Super Spy?"

His arm is around my shoulder. I become aware of how close he is to me and stop talking.

"We should go," says Noah. "I want to eat before the movie—"

I lock down my station, tell Alec good-bye, then ask if he'd like to join us. He smiles but declines, and the group heads outside.

I'm in the parking lot when I hear a rapid car honk behind me. Everyone turns. I catch sight of the Mercedes emblem and the cream-colored car and send up a prayer it's not Farah. The car comes to a stop, and my cousin gets out.

"What are you doing here?" I ask as she comes up to us.

"Your mom said you were working, so I came over."

That's not an answer, that's just more acid for my stomach to chew on. "Why are you here?"

"I came for you."

I gesture to the group. "We're heading out, so . . ."

"Great. Where are we going?"

"We are going to hang out," I say. "You're—"

"Cool. Am I good to leave the car here?"

"Sure," Noah says before I can talk. "Masao won't mind."

"Great, better to carpool and save the environment, right? The car chirps as she locks it. She tucks the fob into her purse. Her bracelets glitter and jangle in the falling dark.

"Ready to go?" asks McKenzie.

"Cool." Noah speaks, and the rest of them echo his word.

The end of the world is coming, not with fire and brimstone and Death riding a horse, but in the resounding chorus of "cool."

They head to McKenzie's truck, but I pull Farah back. "Why are you here?"

"I wanted to talk to you about the NASA trip."

"Not this again—"

"Just think about it."

"Why do you even want me to go?"

"I want to do stuff," she says. "Stuff they'd never let me do. If you're there—"

I wave off the rest of the words because I don't want to hear it. She wants me there as a cover for her to run around and be an idiot, while I entertain the folks at the hotel.

"What do you say? Will you come?"

"I have the audition," I say as I move toward Emily's car. "I'm not missing it for anything."

Thank god that shuts her down. We pile into the back seat, and she makes sure to get in beside Noah. I watch the streets pass me by and listen to her flirt and charm her way into a friendship with him, and try not to be jealous that she can do in twenty minutes what I still wouldn't feel comfortable doing after twenty eons.

CHAPTER EIGHT

SYMPATHY IS A BOOMERANG

Just my luck, Farah decides to not only drive me home but come inside as well. "Aren't your parents waiting for you or something?"

"I told them I was sleeping at your place." She shuts off the car.

Wait. What? "Did you ask my parents if you could?"

She looks at me like I've lost my mind. "Duh."

Farah's sleeping over. When it comes time, I'm putting my parents in a crappy nursing home. In fact, if I can swing it, I'm going to see if I can't make them share a room with Aunty Gul and Uncle Raj. The thought makes me smile as I lead the way to the house.

"Nira." Mom and Dad are in the foyer.

"You're late," says Mom. She notices Farah behind me and relaxes to an at-ease position. "Farah, nice to see you, sweetheart." Mom gives her a hug, then waits as Dad does the same. "Grandma is in the kitchen making tea."

Oh, jeez. More tea.

"Thank you, Aunty." Farah gives me one last look over her shoulder and leaves.

"It's nice to have her here, but you shouldn't use her company as a reason to break curfew," says Mom.

Yep. The crappiest nursing home, ever, is coming their way. I break from them and head to the kitchen.

Grandma has the cups set out and a half bowl of sugar on the table. I take heart at the half bowl. The more sugar, the worse the scenario. Maybe tonight won't be too bad.

"Are you hungry?" she asks. "We have curry and rice."

Both Farah and I tell her we don't need dinner.

"Fine, I'll make you a small plate." Grandma moves to the fridge.

There's a smile on Farah's mouth that mirrors mine. It's weird to think she and I are smiling over the same thing.

Farah thanks Grandma as she sets a plate of food down. Grandma smooths Farah's hair.

I try not to throw a temper tantrum. The mental-parentals talk to Farah, loving her up. I chew my food and choke down my jealousy.

Farah finishes eating and pushes away her plate. "Aunty, Uncle, I want Nira to come to the NASA trip with me."

There goes my appetite. "I told you, I have the audition—"

"But Mac says it's on hold because of the teacher's family."

I don't know what's making me more irritated, Farah not dropping the stupid NASA trip, revealing the audition's been rescheduled, or calling McKenzie "Mac," as though they've been BFFs since pre-K.

"How long is the delay?" Mom asks.

"It doesn't matter. I need the time to practice." Once again, I'm the Incredible Invisible Girl because no one is paying attention to me. Worse, they're talking about me like I'm not even at the table. Before I know what's going on, my parents have agreed for me to take the trip.

The thought of spending four days with Aunty and Uncle Let's List the Ways We're Better than You is a task not even Hercules would take. "Listen—"

"Nira." Grandma points at the food. "Eat."

"But—"

"Eat."

It's not the word, it's the two-word command behind it: Shut Up. I can stare down a lot of people, but Grandma's never been one of them.

It gets worse through the night. Farah parks her skinny butt in between Mom and Dad when we stream a movie. I want a new release, but Dad's all hot and bothered over some eighties comedy with Bette Midler and Danny DeVito. Farah breaks the tie by—no surprise—siding with my dad.

When one of my parents pauses the TV to comment or critique, she acts as though they're the first people to teach her something. She's quick to laugh when they make a joke. If this is what it's like to have a sibling, then I'm glad I'm an only child. I'm also glad she's only staying for one night. Another day and I'd be tempted to shove her down the steps.

Halfway through the movie, I've had enough. I slip away and climb from the basement back to the main floor, and take refuge in my room. What I need is someone to share my troubles. I text Emily and tell her Farah's over. A minute later, the text bings: SO COOL! I'M HERE WITH MAC!

Before I can digest her hanging out with McKenzie, another text comes up. MAC SAYS IF WE'D KNOWN, THE FOUR OF US COULD'VE KEPT HANGING OUT. I HAVEN'T SEEN YOUR FOLKS AND GRANDMA IN AGES!

Hanging out. I mouth the words. McKenzie's never wanted to hang out with me before. Amazing how having a cool cousin can up my street cred. I SHOULD GO, I text back. C U L8R. It sounds abrupt, so I add HAVE FUN WITH MCKENZIE.

When I read U 2! AND SHE SAYS CALL HER MAC, I debate the merits of flushing my phone down the toilet. In the end, I decide to shut it off.

I have no human to share my woes, but music is forever loyal. The new trumpet's there, but at a time like this, I need the familiar friendship of Georgia. I take him out and cradle him on my lap.

"Nira." Grandma's voice comes from the kitchen.

I set down Georgia and go to her.

"Help me make tea."

"God, Grandma, no one needs more tea."

"Put the kettle on."

"We just had two pots over dinner—"

"Fetch me the cups."

Why am I fighting this? I do as she instructs.

She covers her mouth and sneezes.

"You need to see a doctor."

"For a cold? Girl, get some sense."

"Old woman, you first. At your age—"

"Really?"

"Nothing. Sorry, ma'am."

"You're a good person." Grandma reaches into her pocket and pulls out a handful of foil-wrapped chocolate. She hands them to me. "It's nice, what you're doing for Farah."

I pause in the middle of unwrapping the candy. "What am I doing for her?"

"Being nice."

No one can make me behave and be honest like my grandmother. "I'm not nice." I stuff the chocolate in my mouth to sweeten the bitterness of my confession. "I don't like her."

She hands me more candy. "That's why I'm proud of you. Come on, let's go back."

"I'd rather practice." I wait until the tea is made and help Grandma arrange it all, along with a plate of mithai. After I take everything downstairs, I go to my room.

"Don't be jealous," I tell Georgia as I open the case of the new trumpet. "It's just for show. You'll always be my first love."

Georgia has no argument with this.

I take out the instrument and spend a couple of minutes polishing it. That's not only to clean it up and get rid of any previous-renter gunk, but it gives my fingers a chance to learn the feel of the metal curves. I want to play "Hallelujah," and make it sound the way it does on Georgia. As I put the piece to my mouth, Farah barges in.

"You're practicing? Even though the audition's been delayed?" She flops down on my bed.

"It's muscle memory. The more I play, the more ingrained it gets."

"You're so good." She sits up. "I didn't bring any clothes. Can I borrow some sleeping clothes from you?"

Great. My bargain basement polyblends on Miss Natural Fibers. "Sure, but I'm not sure I'll have anything that'll fit—"

"I don't mind if it's a little big."

Why does she say it as though I'm the size of the *Titanic*? I dig through my drawers, looking for the newest and nicest stuff. Trust Farah to hip-check me out of the way and grab for my rattiest pajama set.

"Don't you want something better?" I pull out a serviceable plaid set.

She shakes her head and holds the other shirt close. It's got a faded image of Armstrong. Time's worn down the graphic so it looks like Louis's winking at her. "This one is good. It looks like your favorite."

"It is."

"Then it's perfect."

I'm too tired to decipher why she wants my favorite things. "Why did you sleep over?"

She shrugs. "You get Grandma all the time. She only comes over to our place a couple of times a month."

"She'd come over more if you wanted."

Farah wants to say something—I can tell by the way her mouth falls open. But she closes it, fakes a smile. "It's hard with everyone's schedule. Me coming over here is easier for everyone." She stands and strips off her shirt.

"You wanted to say something else, didn't you?"

Her bra falls to the floor, and her face is buried as she pulls on the pajama top. "Isn't that our life? Wanting to say something but keeping quiet instead?"

"You don't have to stay silent with me." I'm not sure why I'm saying this. Of all the things I want, a close relationship with her is at the bottom of my list.

"Nira. You're so nice."

For the first time, it doesn't sound like trash talk. She finishes changing. I do the same. We go back downstairs. When the movie time's over and Dad's exhausted everyone's patience with eighties movies, we go to my room.

"Will you play something for me?" Farah takes the left side of the bed and crawls under the covers.

Grandma, in the open doorway of my room, stops.

"Sure, but I'm not—" I fumble for the catch on the case. "The trumpet's new, so it may not sound right—"

"Use the old one?" She puts her hands together as though she's praying. "Please? Pretty please?"

My fingers still. Play Georgia? In front of her? I'm not sure I'm ready for that level of intimacy between Farah and me. I'm not sure I'll ever be.

Grandma's watching.

I reach for Georgia. "Any requests?"

"'Black and Blue.' No, wait, 'Till There Was You.'"

"You know Etta Jones's work? I didn't know you listen to jazz." I take Georgia from his case, and Grandma moves off.

"Grams said you love it, and I wanted to know what was so

great about it." She shrugs. "It's not all bad."

Part of me wants to argue with her until she admits jazz is the greatest, but Georgia's in my hands, and the familiar pull starts in my heart. I close my eyes and the first notes of "Till There Was You" start, soft at first, then building.

I want to play the song so it blows Farah's mind. She's better than me in almost everything. This is the only thing I have that's mine over hers. But it's more than competitiveness. She thinks jazz is okay. I want to play so well, she has to change her opinion from good to amazing.

When I'm done, Farah leans into the pillow and sighs. "They'll be crazy not to take you."

"Thanks."

"You don't have to say it with such surprise."

"No, I guess—I guess it's the nicest thing you've ever said to me." For a second, I think she's going to cry, but that would be stupid. I chalk it up to the late night. "Give me a second, I have to clean it, then I'll come back."

Grandma comes out of her room when she hears me in the hallway. She cups my chin and kisses my cheek. "Good girl." Then she moves to my room and my cousin.

I clean Georgia in the bathroom because it would gross out Farah to see the spit valve at work. When I get to the bedroom, she's lying on the pillow, her dark hair spread out like bird wings.

"I'm sorry," she says to the ceiling. "I'm sorry it surprises you when I'm nice." She sits up and gives me an unsure smile. "But I think I should get some credit for being nice, considering who my parents are."

I laugh. "You get extra credit for that," which makes her laugh, too. "Your parents aren't so bad."

"I didn't think it was possible for you to lie."

"Your dad can't be all bad. He came from Grandma, right?"

"She knows what he is." Farah's back to talking to the ceiling. "We all do."

"Don't worry about them tonight." I crawl into bed, unsettled by how well we've gotten along. Farah's being nice and I see the glimmer of what might be if we become friends. I shut off the light, feeling good.

"Hey, Nira? Noah's cool. He's cute, too."

And there goes my good feeling.

CHAPTER NINE

DECEPTION IS A PANE OF SHATTERED GLASS

My parents attack the NASA trip, my school, and work with a ferocity last seen during the Manhattan Pro-ject. In the end, I get time off from school and work. The day before I leave, I'm with Emily and Mac in the cafeteria.

"It's going to be so cool! Scientists and space shuttles." Emily splits her grilled chicken in half and hands it to Mac.

I shouldn't be jealous since she had two sandwiches and shared the first with me, but I want to slap the bread out of my rival's hands. "It won't be."

"Because of your aunt and uncle?" Mac shakes her head. "Farah and I were talking about them last night. They're something else."

So is my life. Who knew it was possible to feel wild and free, yet claustrophobic and trapped at the same time? Farah's doing a great job playing the charming princess, so much so, I'm starting to feel like the evil queen. It's wrong to resent her presence with the gang, but she has friends of her own. Loads of them. Why shadow me and mine?

I feel like the NASA trip was a payment. She gives me a ticket, hotel, and food, and somewhere in the fine print, I allow access to my friends and my life. The worst part is that there's no one to talk to about it. Maybe Grandma, but right now she's at Farah's house. Plus, it feels weird to ask her to take sides between us—especially when I only have to look at her face to see how much she loves Farah.

"I e-mailed Mr. Nam," I say. "But he says he's not sure when he'll do the auditions."

"It has to be soon," Mac says, "otherwise there won't be enough time to practice before the competitions."

"In a way, it's good news." Emily puts her hand on mine. "At least it won't happen during your trip."

True. And that frees me up to concentrate on the bigger problem. Not giving in to temptation and strapping Farah and her folks to the nearest space shuttle, then sending them to Jupiter.

———◇———

The entire family comes to the airport to drop me off. I hug Grandma and whisper, "Sure you don't want to take my place?"

She squeezes me tight. "Not for all the tea in China."

Farah and her parents are waiting for us at the terminal. There's an awkward hug between Grandma and Uncle Raj, an even more awkward one between her and Aunty Gul. When it's Farah's turn, she holds Grandma tight. They whisper in each other's ears until Uncle Raj pries them apart and says we need to leave. Mom makes me share my phone location with Farah, in case we get separated. I do, then make a mental note to shut it off as soon as we're on the plane.

We get to the check-in desk, where my uncle asks for a first-class upgrade. I'm basking in the luxury until I realize the upgrade is only for him.

"My back," he tells the airline rep. "It needs the extra support."

Apparently, so does his ego.

Farah makes me take the middle seat in between her and Aunty Gul, then spends most of the flight sleeping on my shoulder.

"Things are good?" Aunty Gul asks.

"Yes."

"School is okay, too?"

I nod. "I'm an A student, all the way."

"And work?"

I'm starting to see why her marriage was arranged. How many ways can I say my life is fine? "Everything is great."

Her smile is more plastic than the dinner tray in front of me. "How about you?"

"Good."

I cast around for an attendant, hoping they're coming down the aisle with drink, food, or anything else I can put in my mouth to end the conversation. The corridor is empty, just like my brain when it comes to holding Aunty Gul's interest. "You were volunteering with—"

"The nonprofit."

I'd have preferred a specific answer, but on this expedition, I'm the girl Indiana Jones. Instead of a whip, I have a dull spoon and a dull subject. "Do you find it enjoyable?"

She closes the window shutter against the rising sunlight. "We work with community stakeholders to ensure resources are directed to appropriate avenues."

The meaning of the words is lost on me, but the job doesn't sound like fun. The fact she didn't answer my question isn't lost on me, either. I heft my spoon and dig again. "Do you work with donors or community advocates?"

She nods. "I network with a diverse group of people. We synergize our resources to facilitate a granular approach so we can hit the ground running."

She's not the only one who'd like to hit something and run. I put down my spoon and pick up my headphones.

A few hours later, the plane touches down. In what feels like a lifetime later, a red-coated bellman opens the limo door. Uncle Raj leads the way to the front desk. I try not to gawk at the chandeliers, vases of flowers, and marble floors. Farah and her mom take a spot at one of the seating areas, and I join them.

"This will be exciting," I say. "We get to see one of the launch pads and the balloon office. We even get a private talk with one of the astronauts."

This is met with an underwhelming response. Aunty Gul's smile barely touches her lips. Farah twirls her finger in the air, then goes back to texting.

"Here are your keys." Uncle Raj materializes at my left and hands me a room card. "You are on the eighteenth floor with Farah." He holds out a key to his wife. "We're on the twenty-fourth."

"Separate rooms?" I ask.

"Kids need their privacy," he says, "and parents need solitude."

Wow. I'd never get that kind of freedom if I traveled with my family. Come to think of it, I don't even get that privacy at home, and I have a room of my own.

Aunty Gul puts her hand on my shoulder. "Remind me, your grandmother gave me something for you."

I hold out my hand to take it, but she walks away, toward the front desk.

Uncle Raj reaches into his wallet and gives Farah a bunch of money. "For incidentals. Anything else, you have the credit card."

Double wow and a hard swallow to push down the envy.

"Nira, you charge your things to the room."

"You're so lucky," I tell Farah when we break off from her folks and get into the glass elevator.

She looks at me as though I'm dumber than sheet rock and we continue the elevator ride in silence.

Farah doesn't seem impressed with the room but this is my first time in a hotel, and I'm trying not to squeal. Giant beds covered in crisp, white linen and draped with thick pillows. The bathroom has miniature bottles of everything—lotion, mouthwash, shampoo— plus shoe wipes, makeup-removing towelettes.

"Which bed do you want?" She calls from the main area.

The TV is in between the beds, so I tell her it doesn't matter.

"Have the one by the balcony. The night air makes me cold."

I wait until she's in the bathroom before I go tourist and take a million pictures of the pool and ocean. After I pick the ones I like best, I text them to Noah and Emily. They reply that I'm "so lucky to be there!" which I love, and "Tell Farah hey," which I love less.

"What do we do now?" I ask Farah when she comes out.

She shrugs. "What do you want to do?"

"Don't we have to meet for dinner with your folks?"

"These trips Dad calls mini-vacations from reality. As long as I don't get pregnant or arrested, I'm on my own."

The freedom overwhelms me in a heady rush. "What about tomorrow and the NASA tour? They'll want to be there, won't they?"

"No, and if they change their minds, I'm screwed."

I sit on the edge of my bed, remind myself it's all mine, and bounce to the middle. "What are you talking about?"

"We're not going on that stupid tour."

"What!"

She grabs the remote and flicks on the TV. "We'll tell them we're going and do something else instead."

The room tilts.

"Mom and Dad won't question it."

I'm not sure if I'm awed by her bravado or terrified I've been pulled into her deceit.

"We'll do something else."

"My parents think I'm getting some kind of educational trip, we have to go!"

"Calm down, Girl Scout. We'll get some brochures from the lobby and look at some astronaut videos, and it'll be cool. Your parents will never know."

"I'll know, Farah, and I can't do that." Oh my god, I'm trapped in an unfamiliar city with a lunatic and two negligent adults.

"You can't lie to your parents?"

"No."

"Who the hell are you, Clark Kent's illegitimate sister?"

"It's not—Mom and Dad have never lied to me. I can't do it. They'd know." Besides, if I lie now, they'll think I was in on it from the beginning. I'm going to be grounded until forever. Every day I'll wake up and Dad will be at the foot of my bed, lamenting how he ended up with a child who tossed herself in the gutter.

"Oh my god, Nira. Just go with it. If you tell your parents, they'll tell mine, and I'm dead meat."

"Why would you even do this?" Why am I even asking the question? I know the answer. Because Farah is selfish, because she thinks I'm a goody-goody, and because this was probably her way of pranking me. Stick Nira in a lie and watch her twist.

"Because I won, and only a loser would take the tour!"

My insides go cold. "Thanks for calling me a loser."

"Calm down. I didn't mean it like—"

I stand. "What I don't understand is why you asked me to be part of it. You could have asked any of your Farahbots—"

The skin on her face tightens.

"—and they would've lied for you and partied with you."

"I thought you'd be cool."

Cool. "Tell me again you didn't call me a loser." I head for the door.

"Where are you going?"

"Anywhere but here."

I take my key and leave her. Florida's gone from an adventure to a thing to survive. Everything seems dangerous and cold, and I don't have the courage to cross the street and sit on the beach.

I remember the package Aunty Gul has for me from Grandma, so I go to the front desk. Maybe there's something in the envelope that will help me out of this situation, like a check for a million dollars. Or a heavy club I can use to brain Farah.

I tell the clerk my room number. "My aunt and uncle are here, too, but I don't know their room number. They're under Ghani."

He goes to the computer for answers. "Do you want Mr. or Mrs. Ghani?"

"Sorry? I mean, does it matter? Aren't they in the same room?"

"No. Mrs. Ghani is on the twelfth floor. Her husband is on the twenty-fourth."

Whoa. Talk about a vacation from reality. "Mrs. Ghani's room—no, never mind." They didn't tell me about sleeping separately. "I'll see her at dinner."

I help myself to brochures on NASA, taxis, and shuttles, and go to the indoor pool. The place is decorated with soothing blue walls, white columns, and a glass roof. Padded lounge chairs line the pool, and the entire thing gives off a peaceful, zen vibe. I nod at a trio of senior women simmering in the hot tub and sit in one of the chairs farthest from them. It faces the wall-to-ceiling window and gives me a clear view of the beach. For a second, I imagine myself there with Noah. But fantasies of hanging out with low-maintenance friends will wait until I figure out how to untangle myself from this mess Farah put me in.

I have money in my account, which means I can pay admission and take a tour. Mom and Dad don't know the specifics of the educational part of the trip, only that it included a talk with an astronaut. On the NASA website, they have lectures for the public by an astronaut, so I'm covered.

Spreading out the brochures, I take a breath and calculate the cost of the tour. Then I do the math on how much I'll pay a taxi to take me to NASA, and how much it'll cost to feed myself for the day. The estimate spikes my heart rate. It's going to take a giant bite out of my funds. I suppose it's okay because I'm renting the trumpet and I'll have enough left over until the next paycheck, but I had a plan, and Farah's messed it up.

I want to text Emily, but she's been spending so much time with Mac I'm not sure there's space for me. I opt for Noah. It's weird to be in a friend threesome with him and Farah, especially since it's obvious to me who he likes and who he really likes. But I need someone to give me some perspective on not killing her, and he seems a sensible choice.

We go through the usual stuff, at the hotel and it's gorgeous. He asks how the flight was, and a noncommittal food was good, no turbulence works. Or so I think, until the text bings, HOW CLOSE ARE YOU TO WANTING TO KILL THEM ALL?

My laughter echoes in the pool room and makes the old ladies in the hot tub twist my way. I wave an apology. TOO LATE. THINK

HOUSEKEEPING WILL BELIEVE BLOOD IS KETCHUP?

SURE, IF YOU CALL IT CATSUP.

Why can't I be back home with him?

I'M GUESSING FARAH'S BEEN CAUGHT.

My fingers hover over the keyboard. CAUGHT?

YOU KNOW WHAT I MEAN.

???

HOW'S THE "PLAN" FOR THE TOUR?

Holy crap. SHE TOLD YOU?

WANTED MY ODDS ON HOW MUCH YOU'D FREAK OUT.

AND YOU SAID?

BRING A BULLET-PROOF VEST

My head is spinning with the news. Noah knew. He knew, and he didn't tell me. WHY DIDN'T YOU TELL ME? My fingers hover over the keyboard. I want to ask the question again, and follow it up with now I'm stuck in an expensive hotel, my parents will never believe I wasn't in on it, and this could cost me jazz band.

But there's no way to say any of that without sounding like a petulant baby.

IT WASN'T MY PLACE, he texts back. SHE CAME TO ME IN CONFIDENCE, AND I PROMISED I'D STAY QUIET.

Subtext, Noah's chosen Farah over me. I'm glad I'm far away from the older women. They can't see the tears in my eyes.

I TOLD HER IT WAS A BAD IDEA, he continues. I TOLD HER TO BE STRAIGHT WITH YOU.

I need to get him off the screen. THANKS, ANYWAY. I SHOULD GO. SHE'S PROBABLY WONDERING WHAT I'M DOING. TOOK OFF ON HER.

The text bubble appears on the screen, but I click off and shove the phone in my pocket. I stand and stumble from the pool room. Behind me, I hear the old ladies laughing, and it sounds like they're laughing at me.

Stupid Nira, believing she could ever be one of the golden ones.

Idiot Nira, for thinking she could ever compete with her cousin.

My phone buzzes and bings. Noah, probably, but I ignore it. I push out in the street, raising my hand against the blinding sun. A few blinks later, my eyes adjust to the crystal blue sky, and the riot of color on the streets.

I don't even know where I'm going. Don't even know how safe it is to walk around. Is this like home, where there are grids of safe and not-safe blocks? Or is it like other big cities where one block is safe and one block isn't, so it's always best to take a cab?

I don't have money for a taxi, and I couldn't sit still, anyway. The street looks safe. Loads of tourists and stores catering to them. I head left, concentrating on the buzz of people talking, the drone of the traffic, and the shrieks of the seagulls overhead. The wind carries the scent of the ocean. I'd love to go and get my feet wet. But the way I'm feeling, I'll probably walk into the Atlantic and keep going until the ocean is over my head, and I'm too far from shore to be rescued.

I walk and walk until my feet are tired and a sheen of sweat and humidity covers my skin. And I keep walking. I don't know how far away I am from the hotel when I see him, not sure how long I've been walking when it happens, but I'm in the middle of the street when I spot him.

Uncle Raj, sitting on the patio of a bistro. Which is no big deal, except he's with a woman. I'm trying to convince myself she's a client, but when he slips his tongue into her mouth, the denials fall away.

Farah's words come back, about the separate vacation, and now I understand why he's got a different room than Aunty Gul. The questions crowd each other: Does Farah know? Does Grandma? How long has this been going on? Each question shrieks louder than the last. I stumble back, knowing I was never to see this, afraid of the conversation if he spots me.

"Nira."

Farah's in front of me, and for a second, I think I'm hallucinating. This is all a terrible dream, a wretched nightmare, and I'll wake up. But she's solid and real as she blocks my path, as she grabs my arm. "What's wrong with you?"

"How did you find me?" I croak the question, think of what's waiting for her on the other side, and I can't risk her seeing her dad. If she doesn't know, this will kill her. "Never mind. Let's go back. I'm hungry."

"We shared locations on our phones at the airport." She remains immobile. "When you didn't come back, I went to find you."

"Okay, okay." I push her. "Let's go. We can talk it over in the room." I take her arm, yank her, but she pulls away.

"Let's go. The pool is nice." I shove her in the opposite direction from where her dad and his mistress sit, but Farah whirls aside.

"What's your problem?" Her gaze goes from me to whatever is over my shoulder.

The world stops, and I can't breathe as she scans the landscape, her eyes tracking, tracking, track—stopping. Locking.

"I'm sorry," I whisper, not sure if she can hear me, wondering if she hears the same roaring in her ears that I do.

Slow-motion horrible, her gaze slides to me, and she stares at me for a long time. I'm still not breathing. The gears of her brain are whirring, I can feel it, but I don't know what they're processing. And I don't know how to ask her.

Farah's face is shifting, tightening. I know she's trying not to lose it in front of me, but I don't know why. Did she always know and she's embarrassed? Did she never know and now she's shattered and humiliated? How do we pick up the pieces? How do we go on knowing the things Uncle Raj purchases aren't out of love, but that he's buying off his wife and daughter?

And the biggest question looms over me. "Are you okay?" As soon as it's out of my mouth, I realize what a stupid question it is. Of course she's not okay.

The tightness in her face shatters, and her makeup, her perfect hair, her perfect clothes, can't cover her vulnerability. She looks so small and young and easily broken, and I wonder if this is the girl that Grandma sees whenever she looks at her.

Farah spins from me, walking, walking, then running—speeding—from me. I don't bother chasing her. Our conversation is in the rapid footfalls as she pulls away and increases the distance between us. I head back to the hotel.

"Nira, are you Nira?" The guy at the front desk calls my name as I step into the cool of the foyer.

I nod and go to him.

"Your aunt left this," he says. "She said it's from your grandmother."

I take the envelope. In the elevator, I turn it over and over in my hands, hoping there is a magic solution to all I've seen, to all that's happened. The elevator bings on my floor. I step out, pause, and rip open the sacred seal. I unfold the paper, catch the objects wrapped inside it, and read the note. *Have some tea.*

CHAPTER TEN

RECONCILIATION IS A REVERSIBLE COAT

Farah's not in the room. I use the tea bag Grandma put in the envelope to make a cup. I let it steep, then douse it with the creamer and sugar she included. I don't want to text Farah, mostly because I don't know what I would say. But as the minutes tick up, I get worried.

I take out my phone. Noah's texts are on the notification screen, but I can't bother with them now. I unlock my cell and search for Farah. The app says she's in the hotel, and I wonder if she's in the pool room.

I wait, try to watch TV and fail, then try to lose myself in the activities on the street and fail. The minutes become an hour, then an hour and a half. I'm starving, but what do I do?

Uncle Raj said to charge everything to the room, but am I allowed to eat without Farah? It feels like such a stupid question, but he's the kind of guy who would get mad if I stepped wrong, the person who would say, "I'm paying. You eat when I tell you, and only eat when one of my family is around to make sure you're not wasting my money."

Dad's words about money haunt me. I wish I hadn't spent so much on clothes. Looking cute is all well and good until you're starving. Grandma would know what to do. She could give me permission to spend Uncle Raj's money. But if I call, Mom and Dad will want to talk to me. I'm terrified everything I've seen will come gushing out of my mouth.

In the end, I shove my phone in my back pocket and head downstairs. I have enough money for soup, and that'll have to do. But when I get to the restaurant, Aunty Gul is there. For a minute, I watch her, the tight set of her shoulders, the hard line of her mouth, and I wonder if there was ever a time her lips were soft from laughing, if her shoulders ever shook because her body couldn't contain the joy inside.

I go to the table. Her gaze flicks my way. "Sit. I'm going to eat." She doesn't ask about Farah, and I don't say anything.

I listen to her order her dinner—salad, no dressing, no croutons. Salmon, poached only, no spices. Rice on the side, no butter. And I feel like a rebel when I order the clam chowder and the chicken alfredo, and agree when the waiter asks if I'd like extra cheese and garlic bread.

Dinner is silent, and we're halfway through when Farah comes. She sits beside me, takes my garlic bread. I split my pasta with her, one plate, two forks. Aunty Gul doesn't ask where Farah's been, doesn't ask about the day. When it's done, and Farah and I have shared the last of the New York–style cheesecake, I stand and go to the room by myself because Farah says she needs to talk to her mom.

Curiosity is acid-on-fire, and it's burning through me, but I don't say anything. I climb in my pajamas, brush my teeth, and crawl into bed. After I turn on the TV to something mindless, I check in with Mom and Dad, text them to let them know everything is good.

There are endless questions about the flight, the food, what about the hotel and the room. Then there's the question I'm dreading.

HOW ARE GUL AND RAJ?

It takes me a second to come up with the answer. HOW DO YOU THINK? ;-)

That gets an LOL from them, as well as BEHAVE AND BE RESPECTFUL. THEY'RE BEING GENEROUS WITH YOU.

We text for a bit more, then I sign off. I do a lap around the room, then open the text thread I've been avoiding. Noah. I take a breath and read them.

NIRA?

I KNOW YOU'RE PISSED, BUT SHE HAD HER REASONS. TALK TO HER, OK?

CHECK IN WITH ME, 2. I WANT 2 KNOW YOU'RE OK.

I text back. I'M GOOD. SO IS SHE. UR RIGHT. SHE HAD HER REASONS.

The text bubble forms immediately. U WANNA TALK?

NOT ON TEXT. MAYBE WHEN I GET BACK?

IT'S A DATE, SUPER SPY.

I doubt it, but I'll take what I can get. I shoot him a smiley face, get a couple in return, then shut down the app.

Farah's still not back. I do my best to stay up, but between the flight and the stress I'm tired to my bones. I turn off the TV and climb into bed.

I'm not sure when Farah gets in. Sleep fog surrounds me as I hear her in the bathroom, changing. The sheets of her bed get pulled back. I'm falling into the ether when I feel the shift on my mattress. Farah climbs in. Then she wriggles closer. Closer.

I turn and, moving to her, put my arm around her waist. She holds my hand.

I whisper, "I'm sorry," even though I'm not sure what I'm apologizing for—her dad, her life, knowing her secrets. "I'm sorry."

Her breath shudders, her shoulders heave, and I know she's trying not to cry. I hug her tight and say nothing.

———————◇———————

The sun's streaming through the window when I wake up. Farah's sleeping on her back, her mouth wide open, her makeup smeared across her face and pillow. When I get out of the shower, she's awake and rummaging through her suitcase. I notice she's wearing my pajamas.

"You said you were going to throw them out," she says, "but they're still good, so I took them."

"They're literally worn through. I can see through them."

"They're your favorite, and I like them." She pulls the shirt to her nose and inhales. "It smells like your mom's curry." She inhales it again, closing her eyes as if savoring every spice. Farah climbs out of bed and heads to the shower. It takes her an hour to get ready.

"I'm sorry." We head to the restaurant for breakfast. "I should have been honest about what I was doing about the NASA thing." She punches me on the arm. "But you shouldn't have taken off. You scared me. It was lucky I could track your phone."

"I told Noah I was going for a walk."

Her eyes go wide. "That's helpful, you know, because he's on the trip with us. God, Nira, you can be such a ninny. You should've told me."

"No, but I figured he'd tell you—"

That gets me an eye roll. "Noah is a one-way street, doofus.

Whatever you say goes in, but it doesn't come out."

"Yeah, but I thought—"

She rolls her eyes, and I shut up.

After breakfast, Farah says, "We're going to the space center."

"I thought—"

"God, Nira, for once, stop thinking."

We take a cab to Cape Canaveral. When it comes time to pay, for a brief second, I envy her, the money they have. Something happens to Farah and me, somewhere between us stepping into the building and showing our passes. We forget about our parents, Noah, and the Farahbots, and I leave my worries about Emily at the door. It's just my cousin and me, giggling about pooping in space and how much we'd miss ice cream.

Farah and I wander around, taking pictures of the rockets, doing the virtual landing of the shuttle, and listening to an actual astronaut, Dr. Scott Parazynski, talk about his experiences. I'm not sure if I'll tell my parents about him. They already think I don't push to my potential. The last thing they need to know is about a guy who's a medical doctor, went to space, and climbs mountains when he's not scuba diving.

Halfway through the tour, I turn to her. "Let's bail and do something else." We spend the rest of the day touring Cape Canaveral, eating food from the street vendors, and window shopping. When we head back to the hotel, my bag is stuffed with brochures and a purse Farah bought me. She leans her head against my shoulder as we sit in the back of the taxi, and I can tell from the rhythm of her breathing that she's asleep. I wonder if it will be like this from now on, us getting along, or if reality will push in and separate us.

We're sitting outside, at a café close to the hotel, enjoying the wind and the breeze when Farah says, "It's been happening since I was a kid." She uses her tongue to catch a dollop of hot fudge dripping from the spoon.

"What?"

"My dad cheating on Mom." She's so matter-of-fact about it that I almost believe she doesn't care. "He says in a lot of cultures it's commonplace. The man has a wife and a mistress. He didn't like it when I pointed out there was a difference between having a designated mistress and having a series of hookups like he does."

"Doesn't your mom care? Don't you?" I'm afraid to ask the questions. I don't want to break the fragile bond between us, but my curiosity is proving too much.

She heaps a giant spoon of ice cream and nuts in her mouth, slowly chews and swallows. Then her gaze drops as she scoops up a second serving. She catches my eyes for a second, then goes back to watching her dessert. "I didn't know any different. It was normal for him to bring the women home."

The ice cream turns sour in my stomach.

"Then we got here, and—" She swallows some sundae. "I saw your dad and your mom." She pauses, as if reliving the moments with my parents. Then she digs to the bottom of the dish, upending a cherry. "And I realized not every kid lives like me. What Dad's got going on isn't normal."

I take a spoon of ice cream and ponder what her life must be like when there's no protection for her because someone's witnessing the Raul and Gul show. Grandma's visits must be like a break from hell for Farah.

"The weird thing is the more Dad indulges in his women, the more my mom denies herself. As though, somehow, the two actions will cancel each other out. Like not eating carbs makes up for his so-called conferences."

I don't even know what to say. Nothing in my life has equipped me to deal with the bombshell of a serial philanderer, let alone him being my uncle.

"It's okay." She points to my face. "You look like you're in pain trying to think of what comes next, but it's fine. This is just my life."

"But it's not fair," I tell her, loud enough to catch the attention of the other patrons in the restaurant. "What about the long-term damage? What about when you get married? This can affect the kind of guy you choose."

She becomes evasive. "I don't worry about that; I have a plan."

Something tells me she's thinking of Noah, and there are splinters in my heart when I think of her and him together. I feel like a jerk. If anyone deserves some happiness and a good guy in her life, it's got to be Farah, but I'm conflicted. I want her to be happy, but I don't want to pay for her happiness. "I'm just saying, stuff like this can impact your growth and development."

She laughs, chokes on her food, and punches her chest to clear her airway. "God, Nira. You're so good. My long-term growth and development? What are you, seventy-five?"

"I took psychology last semester. They said—"

"Only you would worry about the future me." She tucks a lock of hair behind her ear and gives me a soft smile. "Like yesterday on the street. Trying to get me to go the other way so I wouldn't see my dad because you didn't know I already knew." She reaches across and takes my hand, and the wind sweeps her hair. "You really are the sweetest person I know."

"You asked me why I did this, forcing you on the trip." She takes a breath and gives me an unsure smile. "I wanted to hang out with you, but there are always people around. Mom and your mom, fighting over food and weight. Dad and your dad, fighting over possessions and whose kid is the best. I thought if I could get us away—maybe we could be friends, maybe even a real family." Her face darkens. "But you can never get away from your life, can you?"

"I'm happy to be away from the Farahbots."

"Them." She rolls her eyes.

"If you don't like them, why hang out with them?"

"They're the kids of Dad's clients. I have to play nice, or he doesn't make money. But all those girls talk about is stupidness. Boys and clothes and drinking. It's fine, but can't we talk about other things as well?"

"Like what? Pooping in outer space?"

She laughs. "Or maybe how a guy should treat you, rather than what kinds of dirty stuff you can do to him."

"I wouldn't know about any of that," I say, and feel young and foolish.

"You wouldn't. You'd never sell yourself short for a guy."

I've never been given the opportunity to make the decision, but I don't tell her I've never been asked out.

"Your friends are fun. I like them."

"But we're not talking about saving the earth or thinking about anything big." I think of McKenzie. "Half the time, I'm not sure we're thinking at all."

"You guys have fun, actual fun, with each other. You're not mean about other kids or anything."

"You don't have to hang out with those girls. There have to be other kids at school."

"It's not that easy." She reaches over, helps herself to my bowl of ice cream. "I have obligations to my family. We're brown, Nira—you know it's always about family when you're brown."

"Yeah, but—"

"I have to hang with them. It's connected to Dad's business. If I don't, then it means less money—"

I'm about to open my mouth, play Nira the Conscience and tell her money isn't everything.

"—and if he's not making a certain amount, he gets mad. Me, I can handle it, but it tears Mom apart. I may not like my mom, Nira, but I love her. I have to do what I can to help. Sometimes it's easier to do the thing everyone expects you to do rather than fighting for the thing you want to do." She traces a path between the melting ice cream. "Besides, I'm queen to the Farahbots. It's nice to be worshipped, even if you can't stand your subjects." She won't meet my eyes. "I'm not like you, Nira, I'm not good. I don't like those girls, but I like being in their spotlight." She digs in the dish for more ice cream. "That's why I like hanging out with you and your friends. You make me feel like I'm a decent person."

"You can hang out with us anytime you want." The words are out of my mouth before I realize I'm even speaking them. I'm coming from a place of pity rather than logic. Even as they disappear into the air, I'm regretting them. I'm already having problems with McKenzie taking Emily, Noah liking Farah. The crystal ball says in three months, they'll be together, and I'll be home alone. But the words are out. I can't take them back, no matter how much I want to, and it makes me feel miserable on all levels.

"Super Spy," she says wistfully. "You have an actual nickname. I've never had one."

I force a smile. "We can give you one. Space-pooper."

She laughs. "Gross. I'll wait until we get home. I bet Noah will give me one."

And I go back to being miserable.

———◇———

The day we leave, Uncle Raj is at the front counter, waiting. I haven't seen him since the moment on the street. Try as I might, I can't stop my contempt from rising.

"Had a good time, Nira?" He's joviality incarnate, bouncing on his toes, and rubbing his hands together.

"Yes, thank you for your generosity." I set down my suitcase.

"No problem, no problem. Let your dad know." He claps me on the back.

I recoil.

He's staring, shocked and unsure.

Uncle Raj isn't the only one on shaky ground. I'm not supposed to know any of the things I know. Aunty Gul looks at me like I've lost my mind, but Farah's face would win her a poker tournament. "I'm sorry," I gulp the words. "You took me off guard."

He moves to me, but I step back. His eyes narrow and he squints at Farah. She flips her hair and crosses her arms.

I force myself to put my hand on his shoulder. "I'm jumpy today. I had a bad night."

He nods, but he knows I know. I see his awareness in the light in his eyes. Same with Aunty Gul. Her gaze slides to Farah. They think Farah told me, and I'm powerless to correct them. If I open my mouth, I can't fake ignorance anymore.

This is going to come back and cost me, but I don't know how to avoid his coming wrath. The ride to the airport is silent, and after we check in, Uncle Raj and Aunty Gul disappear. One heads to the bar. The other goes to the first-class lounge.

On the plane, Farah sticks me in the middle seat between her and Aunty Gul. Then she puts in her earbuds and pulls on her sleep mask.

I poke her in the ribs and hiss, "I know you're faking it. Don't leave me alone with your mom."

Farah rolls away but makes sure I see the middle finger she gives me.

I opt to follow in my cousin's footsteps. My fingers fumble to plug the headphones into the plane's system, but Aunty Gul is faster.

Her hand clamps down on my wrist. "Nira." Her gaze bores into mine. "How was the trip?" She leans close as she finishes the question, and I get a whiff of alcohol strong enough to singe my nose hair.

My mouth is Sahara desert dry and my brain's empty. No way will my aunt confide in me like Farah did. I'm already on her radar. If I reveal that I know her marriage is crap, I'm nothing but a target in the bull's-eye. "The trip was good." I shut up before I start babbling.

"Oh, yes? What did you enjoy?"

That's an easy one. "Cape Canaveral." Then I launch into a five-minute oral essay on the workings of the space shuttle, what it's like for the astronauts. I'm rambling, but I'm aiming for the moment when her eyes glaze over, and she wants me to shut up. Aunty Gul's a trooper, and she hangs on for the ride. When the flight attendant swings by our aisle and asks what she wants to drink and she says, "A double shot of bourbon," I know I've got her on the ropes.

I'm talking about how the astronauts use recycled urine as drinking water, and I'm getting into the gory details when my aunt squeezes my wrist.

"This is all well and good, Nira." She takes a healthy swallow of the alcohol. "But science isn't everything." She leans into me, shoulder to shoulder, as though we're sharing a secret. I'm claustrophobic under her weight.

"This world is hard for colored girls. You have to be twice as good as the men because you're a woman, and three times as good as the white people because you're colored. And you're still only considered half as good as either of them. Sixteen times better, but worth only a quarter of them."

My brain is swimming from her creative math. That or I'm getting drunk off her breath.

"What a woman needs is security. Financial security."

"A good job—"

"A job can come and go. You must do all you can to make sure you have the necessities of life. You and your husband are partners; you bring in the money and provide for each other."

Farah rolls and shifts. Her fingers brush mine.

"You must be together on this." Aunty Gul's nails dig into my skin. "A common purpose."

Farah moves again, and I realize her restlessness isn't from sleep. She's gently holding my hand.

Aunty Gul stares at me. "You understand what I'm saying?"

"Yes," I say, and Farah's grip pulses.

"Good." My aunt releases her talon-grip on me. "Good."

I look down at my fingers, intertwined with Farah's. How often has Farah listened to that lecture? Trade your happiness for things; let your husband sleep around if it means you can get a car that drives itself. I fold my other hand over hers and let my fingers warm her skin.

CHAPTER ELEVEN

CLARITY IS A PRISMED CRYSTAL

Mom and Dad are ecstatic to see me. "It was four days." I struggle for air as Mom crushes me close to her chest. "Not four eons."

"I missed you, I missed you." She layers me with kisses.

"Okay, okay!" I pull free, grateful the airport is empty this early in the morning. Cool air hisses along my skin. Grandma wraps her warm arms around me to hug and kiss me. "Are you feeling better?" I ask.

"I'm always good. The walks are the perfect medicine." She pulls away and presses a piece of chocolate into my hand. "It was good?"

I don't answer because I'm watching as Mom turns her attentions to Farah and gives her a long hug. Farah closes her eyes, presses her face close to Mom, and inhales, and it's like she's a moisture-starved houseplant that's finally been given water.

I turn back to Grandma. "It was good."

Her dark eyes take me in, take in the scene with Farah. "Come, let's go home. I'll make you some tea."

When it's time to go our separate ways, Farah hugs me hard. Everyone takes in the visual.

"You're friends now?" From the tone of Dad's voice, he doesn't seem thrilled. It's like I left to spy on another country, and was turned into one of their patriots.

I shrug, grab my bags, and head for the exit. On the ride home I keep the conversation focused on NASA and the sights in Florida. Once we're home, it gets easier to distract them. Nothing makes my mother happy like watching me eat. I stuff myself silly. The growing stomachache is worth it when my dad presses for information on Aunty Gul and Uncle Raj, and Mom shushes him, saying, "Can't you see she's eating?"

"I should get my stuff in the laundry." I push away from the table.

"Nira," Dad calls me back. "Were your aunt and uncle okay? They treated you well?"

I nod. "Yeah."

"So? That's it?"

I give him my best eye roll. "It's Aunty Gul and Uncle Raj. What else can you say?"

He laughs and waves me off.

I dash to my room, closing the door behind me, and put my hand to my pounding heart. Uncle Raj's secrets are his own, and so are Aunty Gul's. I'll help carry Farah's because she's asked me to, but the whole thing weighs heavy on me.

I have a secret, their secret. It steals the stars from the sky and the light from the moon, and I want to tell Mom and Dad. Not because I want to embarrass my aunt and uncle—I just want to free my parents from the idea that their siblings are better than they are.

There's a knock at my door, and Grandma comes in. "You didn't finish the tea."

"I did," I tell her.

She holds the cup aloft, jiggles it, and makes the liquid swirl.

"I finished my cup of tea," I repeat. "That is the third cup you tried to force down my throat."

"It's good for you."

"You know what else is good? Not having my bladder explode."

She sits on my bed, and the colorful folds of her sari settle. "Tell me about the trip."

"It was good."

"As good as a not-exploding bladder?"

I laugh. "Nothing's as good as that."

Her smile fades, and she pats the spot next to her.

I go to it, reluctant, because she'll pull the secret from me and

I don't want to betray Farah. It feels so weird that I care enough about my cousin to want to protect her from pity and judgment.

"You came back different."

"Airport security will do that to someone."

"Nira."

I shrug. "It was a good trip. You asked me to be nice to Farah, and I was. I—she's not as bad as I thought." I can't help the face I make as I say the words, and Grandma zones in.

"Yes, she is, but I think you see maybe why she is the way she is."

I have no answer, so I shrug again.

"I think maybe you saw things."

The glib response is on my tongue, but I love my grandmother too much to speak the words. Instead, I pull away, go to my suitcase, and forage for the box of chocolate. "I brought you these. Chocolate spaceships."

She takes them. "I'll eat them, and you can play me 'Fly Me to the Moon.'"

"Be careful how many you eat. They make you gassy. Too many, and you'll rocket yourself to the moon."

"What did you see?"

"Nothing—"

"Nira."

"Nothing, just Aunty Gul and Uncle Raj being themselves, okay? And I felt bad for Farah."

There's a long silence as she inspects my face. I turn away, unable to meet her gaze.

"So, you know."

My heart skips. "Know what?"

The look she gives me is pure senior-citizen sarcasm. "That the world is round. You know about Raj, don't you?"

"You know about him, too?" The weight on my chest is lifting. It's a helium balloon carrying me to the ceiling.

"A mother knows her children."

"How can you stand the knowing—doesn't it bother you?"

"He's not doing it to me. His actions are between him and his wife." She stops for a moment to smooth her sari. "I don't like the effects it has on Farah."

"Is that why you go?"

"I would go more often, but he won't allow it. He'd have to behave." She sighs, and for a moment, it looks as though she feels every second she's been alive. "The hardest lesson to learn as a parent is that your children are not copies of you. They are their own people who will make bad choices and mistakes. But if he were still a child—" Her eyes flash.

"I'll make you some tea. Stay here."

She squeezes my hand. "You're such a good girl."

I go to the kitchen, my actions on automatic as I boil the water, my brain mulling it all over. Two boys growing up in poverty, pity, and with the shadows of people's self-satisfaction darkening their steps. They grow into men. I think of my father, quietly saving every penny, denying himself the compromise—the midsize car, the midquality BBQ—because everything he buys will have to be top of the line. Then there's Uncle Raj, having it all but hungry for more, greedy and grabbing, no matter who it hurts.

The kettle boils, and I steep the tea. There must be a compromise, a halfway point between my dad and his brother, but I don't know what it is, and I can't find the light to direct me. The worry niggles at me, the shadow grows, and warns that if I don't find the answer, I'll end up as one of them.

CHAPTER TWELVE

ANGER IS A CHEMICAL BURN

Finding out about my uncle seems to have cursed my life. Everything's going sideways, and I don't know how to stop it. I pretend not to notice how McKenzie saves a seat for Emily, and pretend not to be hurt when Emily sits next to her and not me. McKenzie's territory includes Noah, too. She's always flirting, laughing, touching. The storm's coming, and I don't have an umbrella.

Practicing for the audition is the one solace I have, but even that's not going well. My skills aren't where they need to be, and nothing sounds right. Maybe it's the new trumpet. It sounds and feels different, and we haven't been together long enough for me to give it a name. But it's a poor musician who blames her instrument, and the whole thing sucks.

Mr. Nam finally gives us an audition date and, a couple of days before, Farah and I go to the mall. She helps me pick out an outfit.

She's a mother hen, clucking and *tsking* as she squeezes one eye shut and cocks her head, taking in the ensemble.

"It's just clothing." I'm embarrassed by the level of scrutiny.

"Nothing is just anything." She pulls on the cuffs of peasant blouse. "Especially with you and clothes."

I open my mouth to object. The lecture is on my tongue. Why can't she ever stay sweet? Why does there always have to be a tart aftertaste to everything she says?

"You've got great lines. You're tall and solid, and we want to emphasize all your best qualities." She eyes the denim jacket that falls over the shirt. "The problem is that every part of you is a great feature, so what do we highlight?"

Okay, one of us is an idiot, and it's not Farah. "Oh. Uh, thanks."

"Don't thank me, not until we get this right." She pulls the jacket off. "No, none of this will do. We have to find you something else."

"Can we eat, first? I'm starving."

"Why is it always about food with you?"

"Because I have a psycho cousin who has trotted me around the mall for the last three hours, and she won't let me eat or drink anything."

"What a baby. You think girls wake up looking gorgeous?" The smile plays on the edges of her mouth. "Go on, get dressed. We'll get you some food, and maybe change your diaper."

In the end, we both agree on a pair of tan cowboy boots that make me feel western and sophisticated and rebellious, all at once. I buy a cream tunic that skims my body, turquoise-accented bracelets, and a few long statement necklaces. A pair of skinny jeans completes the outfit, and it's perfect. Chic, hip, and artistic, without looking like it's trying too hard. Best of all, it's from an actual store so Dad won't freak. Farah buys a purse, and it's buy one, get one at a fifty-percent discount, so she gives me the second.

We're heading out of the mall and back to my house because she's sleeping over, when I spot McKenzie and Emily. They see us, too. There's a quick, whispered conversation between them. Emily says something, but McKenzie shakes her head.

My stomach rolls. What is it that Emily wants to say or do? Hang out with us? Tell me she doesn't want to be my friend anymore? A couple of seconds later, they come over. Everyone's talking and laughing. Farah's digging into my bag to pull out the clothes and show them.

"Oh!" Emily squeals. "It's perfect. You're going to look and sound awesome, Nira."

But I'm only half-focused on her words. I'm caught in the weirdness of it all. I wasn't even invited to hang out with Emily and McKenzie. I know I'm with Farah, but that doesn't count. She's family. She's not Emily.

"We're heading to the theater." Emily follows her words with a hard stare at McKenzie. They vibe their conversation.

Instinct says Emily wants us to come along, but McKenzie says, "Yeah, we should get going. It was nice to see you guys." Then she pushes Emily along.

I'm seething, but I don't say anything because there's no way for me to get the words out without sounding like a jerk.

"You okay?" Farah watches me.

"I'm fine. Let's go."

She walks in the shadow of my stony silence. We get to her car. I toss the bag in the back, and suddenly all the brightness is gone from the day. We're a few blocks away from home when Farah says, "What's going on? You got a great outfit. Grandma says you sound fantastic on the new trumpet."

"It's not about that, okay? Anyway, I'm fine. It's all fine."

Farah's hands tighten on the wheel. "Don't do that. You sound like my mother, and I get enough denial at home—"

"Let it go, and stop twisting my life into a spotlight on how hard it is to be you."

She flinches but doesn't take her gaze off the road. "I'm sorry, that's not what I'm—I know something's bugging you. Is it Emily?"

I don't say anything. This is too personal. Farah and I aren't a hundred percent, not yet. I know she's texting Noah, and I'm sure they're hanging out, just the two of them. She's never going to understand how I feel. "Drop it, okay?"

She shakes her head. "No. I haven't—we're doing great, Nira, you and me. I'm not going to let it go. Tell me what's bothering you."

"God, Farah. Drive. We're fine, okay?"

"It's 'cause Emily's spending so much time with Mac, isn't it?"

"Mac." Her name slides from my lips, covered in sarcasm. "Big Mac, all cheesy goodness, looks great, but does nothing for you." I don't mean to spill the words, but the anger and hurt bubbles too close to the surface.

"She's a bit much," Farah says with a laugh. "But she's harmless."

"That's what they said about the Trojan horse." Jeez. Why can't I shut up?

"She's not so bad. Emily still loves you."

Maybe, but it seems like she loves McKenzie even more. There's nothing special about me; Emily can find a new best friend in five seconds. But she's irreplaceable to me.

Farah gives me a soft punch on the arm. "Sometimes you have to share your toys."

The bubbling goes to a full-on boil. "You would say that."

"Me?" She turns her startled gaze my way. "Why do you say that?"

"Because I'm always sharing. When you sleep over, you're in my bed. My clothes—I still don't have back those pajamas. Grandma. Mom and Dad."

"I'd share my family and house." Her voice is straining to stay light. "But my toys are broken and should be recalled for toxic materials."

"And what about my friends?" Before I can stop myself, it's out. "What about Noah?"

"What about Noah?"

"Give me a break, Farah. All the texting, the touching, the food sharing. Isn't it enough that you've hijacked Emily and McKenzie, and my house and my family? You have to take Noah, too? When is it enough for you? Or are you going to keep throwing trips and brand-name bags my way in exchange for my life?"

She blinks fast, and her jaw clenches tight.

We don't talk for the rest of the ride. The blood thrums in my ears and pounds in my veins. But deeper still is the inner voice that wonders why I have to be so like my dad. Why can't I keep my mouth shut, and why do I feel like I'm always setting fire to things that are already smoldering?

She pulls onto the driveway, but when I go to unlock the door, she hits the button and locks it again. Once more, I unlock it, but she revs the engine. The lock snaps back in place.

Farah turns, and her dark gaze is bright with unnamed emotion. "I'm not a dog, Nira, and Noah's not a bone. You don't get to possess people just because you saw them first, and you don't get to be their only friend." She hits the button and unlocks the door. "Get out."

I take my bag and head up the stairs, and I don't look back.

"Where's Farah?" Mom comes into the foyer.

"She went home."

"Home?" Her mom gaze goes into hypermode. "What happened?"

"Nothing, okay?" I kick off my shoes and head to my bedroom, my bag in hand.

"Nira, what happened? Talk to me—"

"I'm sick of talking to people," I say. "I want some time alone."

"I'll make you some tea."

"I don't want—!" I lower my voice. "I don't want any tea. I want to be alone." I go to my room and close the door. Farah's still driving home, but I check my phone anyway to see if she left a text. Nothing.

Good.

I'm tired of always playing nice so everyone else can be happy. It's my time now. I take the clothes out of the bag, rip off the tags, and try not to think of my cousin's smile as she handed me the bracelets.

"Nira?" Grandma's tap at the door follows the question. She opens the door, a cup of tea in her hand.

"Don't start with me, old woman." I point to the cup. "I'm not thirsty."

The side of her mouth twists. "This is my tea."

"Yeah, right."

She holds it out. "Try it. Mine, not yours."

"What does it matter? We both take it the same way."

She lifts it higher. "Try, you'll see."

I take the cup and have a swig. It's hot and sweet.

Grandma makes a face. "Gross, now it has your juju in it. I don't want it, anymore. You drink the rest, don't let it go to waste."

Foiled by a senior citizen once again. "I don't want to talk. You love Farah—"

"So do you."

I ignore her words. "I don't want you in the middle."

"I'm already in the middle." She sits on the bed. "Nice stuff. Farah helped you buy them?"

"I have homework, and I should practice for the audition."

"Who's stopping you?"

"You."

Her eyebrows rise. "I take up so much space?"

"You know you do."

She shrugs and stands. For a minute, I think she's going to leave. But she crawls to the top of the bed, moves the pillows, lies down, then covers herself with them.

"What are you doing?"

"Sharing space with the pillows. Now I'm not taking up any room." She coughs, and the pillows jiggle.

"In some places, I could have you committed."

"Good. I believe a person should always be committed to the things they believe in."

"She's taking everything. She's here all the time, and I can't even see my friends without her there."

"Farah?" Her voice is muffled from the pillows on her face.

"No, my invisible friend, Mary the Moose."

"It bears asking. Crazy runs in this family. I heard you have a grandmother who pretends to be bedding accessories."

"Take those off your face." I move the pillows. "I have visions of you suffocating."

She sits up, pats the spot next to her, and covers her mouth as she coughs.

"You should see a doctor."

"Can't. I'm a medical miracle. A doctor looks at me, and all he'll want to do is document my magnificence. His whole career, just me. We're in a health-care crisis; I can't do that to the rest of the people."

"I feel like I'm in crisis."

She hands me a square of wrapped chocolate. "What happened with you and Farah?"

"The same thing that always happens." I punch the pillow and lean back on it. "She has everything, and it's not enough. Now she has to have my friends and family." I stare at the ceiling.

"She's such a pot salt. Sleeping over every weekend, texting Emily, being friends with McKenzie—" Noah's name is on my lips, but I keep quiet.

"And a crush. There's always a matter of the heart involved. Is it a boy or a girl?"

"It's not a crush; it's just this boy. Noah."

"You both like him, and I guess he likes Farah?"

I shrug.

"You like him more?"

"Not like that—it's just different when it's a guy who's your friend, and your cousin's flirting with him all the time. How am I supposed to compete with that?" I pick at my jeans. "She even takes my clothes."

"She wears your clothes, borrows your friends, loves the boy you love—"

"I'm not in love."

The look she gives me is pure snark. "She's using your mom and dad as surrogates, and of course, there's me."

"Of course."

She digs into her robe and hands me a piece of candy. "Put it together. What's the answer to why Farah's doing this?"

The crinkle of the wrapper fills the silence. "I don't know."

"Nira! You are an A-plus student—you don't know the answer?"

I shake my head.

She sucks her teeth and rises as Mom calls us for dinner. I go to the bathroom to wash my hands. When I get to the table, there's a black-and-white photo on my plate. Me, drenched in Grandma's costume jewelry, my feet drowning in her shoes, and her makeup smeared all over my face. "What's this?"

"One of my favorite pictures of you." Grandma sits beside me. "Look at you."

I laugh. "Yeah, I was something all right." I trace the lines of the photo. "I just wanted to be like you—"

Grandma smiles and pats my arm.

Bested by the old lady, once again.

I spend the next two days texting Farah and telling her sorry, but I get no reply. When the day of the audition comes, I'm frazzled and nervous. I burn myself in the shower and cut my legs shaving. Even when I try to take a breath and slow down, I still manage to stub my toe on the dresser.

School is even worse. I have no patience for the McKenzie and Emily show at lunch. I try to hold in the sarcasm, but it's hard, especially when they're sharing their fries and drinks, and giving each other special looks I can't decode. My short temper leaves Emily staring at me like a puppy who's been scolded and doesn't know why.

But there's McKenzie to pat her arm and say, "Don't worry. She's just nervous." Then she shoots me a look full of ill intent.

"You'll do just fine, won't you?"

"Yeah, I'll be fine." I grab my tray and stand. "I'm going to walk around for a bit."

I leave them. The thunder's rolling, the lightning's flashing, and I still don't have my umbrella.

CHAPTER THIRTEEN

RESOLUTION IS A WALL OF BRICKS

I sit in the gym with the crowd of hopefuls, waiting for my turn to get up and play. Mr. Nam is rough, hard-core. He barely cleared my rented instrument for auditions. Now I'm wondering how I'm going to measure up to his exacting standards. Georgia rests beside me, patient and waiting for our time.

Georgia is next to me.

Oh god. I brought the wrong trumpet.

Now I'm staring at the case. I'm such an idiot. The whole point of getting the job and renting from Reynolds was so I didn't walk onstage and embarrass myself and Georgia. I'm still staring at the case, as though I can will it to be the new trumpet.

"Don't sit there like a ninny," says a voice. "Take it out and warm up or something."

I spin around. "Farah!" I stumble to my feet and lock my arms around her neck.

"Chill, weirdo. It's only been a couple of days."

"I'm so sorry. I was such a jerk." I speak the words into her skin and inhale the scent of her.

"God, you're so emotional. It's fine." She pries herself from my grip, but I catch the smile that tugs the edges of her mouth.

"I brought the wrong trumpet," I tell her, and try not to cry.

"The wrong one? Is it broken?"

"No, it's Georgia. I brought Georgia."

Farah shrugs. "It's a trumpet, and it plays. Besides, it's your Georgia. You guys know each other."

"But he's a pocket trumpet." I'm one breath away from wringing my hands or fainting. Maybe both. "Mr. Nam's never going to put me in band if I pull out a pocket trumpet."

"He's never going to have the chance to decide if you don't take out any trumpet."

The clash of cymbals jerks my attention to the front. Everyone's staring at us. Noah's eyes are full of concern and worry. My gaze tracks to Mr. Nam, and he's a symphony of irritation.

"Thank you, Miss Ghani. Perhaps if you're done with your BFF time, you can lend us peasants some of it?"

I'm so glad I'm colored and no one can see me blush. "Sorry, sir."

"Apologies aren't anything but stale air. We've been waiting and calling you. Get up onstage or stop wasting everyone's time."

I grab my case and scurry to my spot, ignoring McKenzie. She's doing something with her hands, but I'm positive it's some blond girl voodoo to mess up my audition.

I get to the stage. My legs are like overcooked spaghetti. This is the moment, and I'm terrified. This is the moment, and I'm petrified he's going to take one look at my trumpet and kick me off the stage. Or that the kids will laugh. Or both.

I didn't think it would be like this. I thought I'd feel powerful and victorious. That, at the least, I'd feel like a conquering hero. Reality is a kick in the crotch.

With shaking hands, I undo the latch. And for a second, that's all I can do. I'm scared into paralysis. My heart stops. The world stops. Then I take a breath and move to the case.

"That's enough," says Mr. Nam. "Next."

I'm sure I've heard wrong. "Sorry?"

"Off the stage, Nira. Time for someone else."

"But I haven't auditioned—"

"You did, and thanks. Now it's time for someone else."

I open my mouth, but the look on his face stops me. I lock the case, and my hands are shaking, but for an entirely different reason. I can't get my fingers to grasp the handle. The next kid is onstage, coming toward me with his sax in his hands, and sympathy on his face.

"I'm sorry," he whispers as he takes my place.

I nod and stumble to the stage exit. Emily is there, her arms open. "I'm so sorry. What a jerk!"

I fall into her embrace, the empty holes inside me filling with her love, but she's not enough to plug all the spaces. This can't be how the story ends. I've worked too hard, sacrificed too much, done too much fighting with Mom and Dad to come back a failure. I'm not going to fall to some teacher who's full of smug self-satisfaction. I breathe the scent of Emily's perfume and come up with a plan.

The gang finds me at the water fountain.

"That was a garbage move." Farah spits the words. "Your parents should complain."

Noah shakes his head. "That's typical of Mr. Nam. He's hard-core."

"How did you guys do?" I ask and get awkward looks from him and McKenzie.

"They got in." Emily waves her hand in dismissal. "The question is how to get you in."

"No, wait. We need to take a second." I hug Noah, which feels awesome, and then I force myself to hug McKenzie, which is way less awesome. "Congrats. We should celebrate. Just because I didn't get in doesn't mean we ignore what you did." The words are hard as cement to get out, but I don't want the focus to be me. And besides, they did good. I don't want to be the person who dismisses their victories.

"We were thinking of pizza," says Noah. "My treat."

"Dessert's on me," says McKenzie, then nudges Emily and whispers something to her that makes her giggle.

My handle on zen-Nira is slipping, and I need the gang gone before I go to pieces. "You guys go ahead; I'll meet you later."

Emily says, "No, first we take on Mr. Nam." She slaps her back pockets. "Okay, first we find my phone, then we take on Mr. Nam."

"Maybe we can start a petition—" Noah.

"I still think your parents should step in—" Farah.

"Maybe a stern letter?" McKenzie, looking constipated at the complex thought.

I hold up my hand. "Guys, it's okay. I'm going to talk to him."

"We'll all talk to him," says Noah.

"No, it's fine, I've got it handled. You guys go ahead. Just text me the address of where you go."

"I'll stay." Farah plants her feet. "You'll need a ride."

"No." I feel like I'm a dim-witted parrot who knows only one word. "No. You go ahead. Maybe you and Noah can carpool?" God, that hurt to say. But she was right—he's not a bone, and we're not a pack of dogs. If he'd rather be friends with her than me, so be it, even if it'll leave me sobbing into my pillow.

Farah blinks and catches the subtext. "Um—okay."

I don't know if she agrees because she loves Noah that much, or if it's because she respects the olive branch I'm holding out.

She takes my hand and squeezes it. "Good luck."

"I don't like this," says Noah. "Mac or I should be with you. We know him better."

"Guys, some dragons you slay on your own." I grin to cover up the nerves. Then I rush them off, still grinning like an idiot. As soon as they're out of sight, the fake emotions drop. The truth is, I'm terrified. I'm not built to argue with adults. Guyanese are all about respecting the elders, but I want a spot in the band. If I have to go toe to toe with a teacher who's scary enough to make me feel nauseous, then so be it.

I heft Georgia, go to Mr. Nam's office, and knock on the partially opened door. "Mr. Nam?"

"Nira. I thought you'd stop by." His back is to me. He swivels in his seat but doesn't stand. "If your trumpet playing is anything like your academics, I bet you're amazing. I'm sorry I won't get a chance to find out."

It's a dismissal, but I'm not moving. Not so much because I'm feeling brave. More like my legs are paralyzed, and Mr. Nam's going to have to call the janitor to wheel me out. "I want to talk to you about my audition."

"What about it? You had your chance. Just like all the other kids."

"No, I didn't. They got to play."

He shakes his head. "No, they got time on the stage, just like you."

"I was nervous—"

"I understand, but I'm not your parent or your therapist. You had your chance on the stage. I'm not responsible for what you did when you were on it."

"But—"

He stands. "Nira, look, I know you think you wanted to be in jazz band, and that's fine. But it's not about want. Lots of people want things. It's about what you do with the want—"

"That's not fair."

"Not fair? You were there to audition. Your mind should have been on the task at hand. Instead, we were left waiting for you to finish your conversation. I called and called you, but your friend was what had your focus, not the audition."

"That's not true. I brought the wrong trumpet—that's what I was talking about."

His bushy eyebrows go up. "You weren't paying attention enough to bring the correct trumpet. Tell me again how much you wanted to be in the band."

"It's not that—" I'm feeling desperate, and I'm sweating through my tunic. "The other trumpet is new. This one"—I lift Georgia's case—"I've had this one forever. It was just habit that made me pick it up."

"So why didn't you use it?"

"I—" I sigh. "It's a pocket trumpet."

"Does it make music?"

I nod.

"Then why didn't you use it?"

My mouth is dry, and my tongue feels like a wad of sandpaper. "I thought—I thought if you saw it, you wouldn't think I was a real musician."

He shakes his head, and the movement is full of sadness. "Nira, are you a musician or someone who just carries an instrument? Music originates from anywhere and everywhere, and it's about what's inside of you coming out as melody, not about how shiny your instrument is."

"I know." I blink back the tears. "That's what I realized, but just as I was reaching for Georgia—my trumpet—you told me to step down."

"You get on the stage, and you have thirty seconds to start playing. It's my rule for auditions. That's what keeps it fair."

"I know, but—" I keep trying to make him understand. I tell him about how much I fought with my parents to get the chance to try out, then fought with them to get the job to pay for the new trumpet.

And all he says is, "Why didn't you bring that fighter's spirt to the audition?"

Then I try to tell him about how nervous I was, how hard I'd practiced and worked.

"It was your moment, Nira, and your fear came through. And that's okay. Sometimes we're scared. It happens. We're human. But a moment comes, and then it's gone. If it was what you're waiting for, you can't hesitate. You have to take it. That's life. If you become a bomb expert, you can't hesitate when it comes to cutting the wires."

I swipe my eyes. "But I'm not a bomb expert—"

"Maybe not, but those thirty seconds were your chance to set it off, and you didn't. Life is about focus, it's about being in the moment. At that time, your job was to be present in the audition, because your job in the band will be to be present for your fellow members."

I want to argue that a moment of hesitation shouldn't disqualify me. That sometimes it's about trying, then failing, then trying again. And I open my mouth to say all those things, when it hits me.

He's here, talking to me while his baby is in the Natal Intensive Care Unit. He was here at the school, listening to the kids audition when the obvious choice was to be at his son's bedside. He's here, with me, calm and reasonable, when I'm sure inside, he's freaking out, and negotiating with any and all the gods that they not take his baby from him.

I hold out my hand. "Thanks, Mr. Nam. You'll see me, again, next year."

He smiles and shakes it.

"Go see your son."

Emotion flickers on his face, and the way he squeezes my hand transmits his gratitude, his hope, and his fears.

I head down the hallway, turn the corner, and almost run into the gang. "What the—didn't I say to go ahead?"

"You say a lot of things," says Farah. "Most of it is just blah, blah, blah."

"Like we'd leave when you were fighting a dragon." Noah throws his arm around my shoulder. "What if you needed a distraction?"

"I'm starving," says McKenzie. "Let's go eat."

"Hey, Emily, wait up."

She waves the rest of the group off and leans against a locker. "How are you?"

"Okay, I guess. It sucks, but that's not what I wanted to talk to you about." Now that we're at the moment, I can't find the words or the courage.

She grins. "Is this our psychic twin thing?"

"It's McKenzie," I blurt out, then start sweating when her smile fades.

"What about Mac?" Her voice is a monotone warning, but there's no getting off this track now.

"I feel like—I feel like I'm being pushed out. We don't hang out like we used to."

"Our group is growing, but we still hang—look at us now. We're hanging."

"Emily, you know what I mean. McKenzie's—"

"Mac. Her name is Mac. Why can't you call her that?"

"Because I don't like her!" I don't mean for the confession to slip out, but the words hang between us, and there's no way to take them back. "She's mean to me. She's always making racist jokes and being snotty."

"Why can't you give her a chance?"

"Why should I? She can't even get my religion right."

"What about you?" Emily faces me. "Do you know what Mac's religion is?"

"What?"

"What's her faith?"

I can't believe she's turning this around so I'm the one at fault. "I don't know."

Emily sighs. "Maybe if you paid attention to her, she'd pay attention to you. Maybe then you'd see she's not all that bad."

What's happening here?

"Come on." She steps away from the locker and starts down the hallway. "They're waiting."

"Emily—"

"Don't make me choose." The rest of the sentence lies unspoken. *Don't make me choose because I'll choose her over you.*

I trail behind her, and when we get to the group, I fake happiness. McKenzie and Emily have a telepathic conversation, aided by side glances at me. All of it does me in. I'm losing Emily, losing Noah, and Farah.

How much longer will I have as part of their group? How much longer until they rid themselves of the pesky fifth wheel? Poetry from English class floats in my brain. The bards sing their sonnets and verses in my ear, reminding me life is about loss, that all good things come to an end. But it's all so unfair. It's ending for me but beginning for everyone else. I choke down my food, say the right things, laugh at the right times, but inside I'm breaking. The storm is here, and I'm nothing but the invisible girl, getting soaked in the rain.

———————◇———————

The conversation at home is what I expect. Mom's at the kitchen table, spinning the cup in her hand, her emotions conflicted. She's ticked at Mr. Nam for not letting me into the band—"You're perfect. What? The man doesn't want to win awards or place first?" But she's also sympathetic to his reasoning—"You need to concentrate, and be prepared."

Grandma says nothing.

Dad's pure happiness. "This trumpet thing was a waste of time, anyway. Now you can go back to studying. Your grades have suffered—"

"A two-percent drop?"

"Your entrance to an Ivy League school lives and dies in that two percent."

"Dad—"

"Nira, you wanted to try out for the band, and you have your answer. The discussion is over." He stands.

"No, it's not. I didn't want to audition for the band; I wanted to play the trumpet. That's what I want, not being a doctor."

"You didn't ask for that, you asked for a band audition, and you got it. The trumpet goes back into the case."

I shake my head. "No, Dad. *This* is what I want."

His face darkens. "We didn't bring you here to end up in the gutter."

"You didn't bring me here to live your dreams, either."

"Don't get fresh with me!"

"I'm not—God, why is it every time I voice my opinion I'm disrespectful?"

Grandma rises and heads to the kettle. Mom's struck dumb, her eyes moving from her husband to her daughter, unsure of who she should side with.

"Because you're disrespectful," says Dad. "This is over now."

I bolt to my feet. "No, that's not fair!"

"Keep going, and I'll take both your job and the trumpet." The skin on his face is tight, and there's a light in his eyes that says he means business.

But I'm his child, stubborn and unable to back down, just like him. "I earned the right to do this."

"You earned nothing. Even your teacher knows. You tried out, and you weren't good enough. It's done." He shoves the chair out of the way and storms off.

"It's not done," I mutter to myself and wave down Grandma as she holds up a cup. "No, no tea."

"Okay," she says, "a small cup."

"No, no I don't want tea. I'm not thirsty and drinking tea isn't going to solve my problems."

Mom takes a sip from her mug.

"Tea solves all problems," Grandma says. "When you're drinking, you can't talk. Sometimes it's good for you to keep your mouth closed."

Mom chokes on her drink.

"Please," I tell my mother, "like you've never said that to me."

"Leave me out of this." Mom walks away.

I watch my grandmother, the hunch of her back, her deliberate movements as she pours hot water into the teapot to warm it up for the tea. "Do you really think I should stop fighting?"

"You think that's what I said?"

"You told me to shut up."

"I said when you're drinking, you can't talk. So, if you can't talk, what else can you do?"

"You know, old woman, your riddles would be a lot more fun if they involved a flying carpet, a temple of doom, some kind of treasure map, or some superhot guy."

"Don't you already have that Noah boy?"

I hide my flush behind my hand. "No, you should provide one of those things, a whip, treasure map, danger—"

She tosses a smile over her shoulder. "Your father's mouth isn't doom enough?"

I laugh. We sit in comfortable silence as she makes the tea. When it's ready, she sits beside me and pats my hand. "What can you do when you're not talking?"

"Stew and fester in the unfairness of my life."

She rolls her eyes.

"Think?"

"Good, now you're using the brains I gave you."

"Don't you mean the brains my parents gave me?"

She raises an eyebrow so high, it almost disappears into her hairline.

I sip my tea and point at the cup. "See? Not talking."

"Was your dream to be in the band?"

"My dream? No, it's what I told Dad. I don't want to be a doctor. I want to be a musician. I'd love to be in an orchestra, but the big dream is to be part of a quartet like Bond or Escala. It would be so awesome to take jazz and blues, maybe even classical, and create something, like what Verve Records did when they put out their Verve Remix collection." I trace the handle of my cup with my finger. I've never spoken that dream to anyone, and speaking it out loud is like being in a cave and having the words echo back.

I'm in the dark and alone, and my heart is pounding, but if I squint, I can see the light, the way to make my dream a reality. "But maybe he's right. It's not like I'm stepping into a field where there's a ton of growth or even opportunity. How many philharmonic orchestras are in the world?" It's a question I've never thought of answering, until now. "Maybe a few hundred?"

"You don't need a hundred jobs; you only need one."

"But the health-care field, science. If I got a doctor's degree, worked in the emergency ward for a few years to get experience, I could flip that into anything I wanted. I bet I could get a job in a resort. I could even create my own business—visit patients in their homes rather than in an office. I could set my hours, pick my clients."

"Maybe you could hum them a tune while you take their temperature."

I squint at her sarcasm.

She meets my gaze with an unerring stare. "Close your eyes; imagine yourself at forty. Will you be happy?"

I do as she asks. "I'd have a decent retirement plan, have worked down my mortgage."

"That's what your father wants for you, financial security, and that's fine. Is it what you want?"

I imagine sitting at someone's house, listening to them tell me about their aches and pains. It's a pleasant image, and I like the idea of helping someone. But when the other picture sneaks into my brain—the one with me under the pink and orange lights, blowing a melody and making the crowd swoon—it takes me to a whole other level. I'm weightless and floating in the dream. "I don't want that. Mom and Dad made it work with not much money. It's what I know and learned, why can't I do that?"

"One day you'll be old, and you'll think of your mistakes and regrets. The biggest ones that will haunt you are the times you could have tried, but you didn't." She takes my hand. "You only have this life, Nira. What will you make of it?"

I take the Reynolds trumpet with me when I head to work. Alec glances at the case as I come through the door. "Upgrading already? Anything left or is it all smoldering metal?"

"Returning."

Concern sweeps across his face. "Something wrong with it?"

"No, Georgia is who I play, and he's what I know."

He nods, then frowns. "Georgia?"

"Sorry, my trumpet. I named him Georgia." It's weird to tell my secret, but it feels good. I survived not getting into the band, telling Grandma my big dream. Calling myself out on what I play doesn't feel like a big deal.

"Cool. What kind is it?"

"It's not a kind; it's a pocket trumpet."

"Really? That is cool. You know, a lot of the professional guys use them during performances."

"Don Cherry did, but he was old-school classic cool. I am not."

"And Patrick Boyle, Médéric Collignon—"

"All well-known, all established enough to do the eccentric thing."

"Yeah, but there was a time when no one knew their name. You just have to play and play until you're part of the establishment."

"Well, that's an easy solution. Why didn't I think of that?"

He takes the case from me. "Because you're a closet instrumentalist. You play, but you'd deny that you're a musician to the public."

It hurts to think that everyone knows how quickly I'd abandon who and what I really am. "Not anymore. I think my dad will disown me, but I got to own this."

"Your dad won't disown you. You're smart. If you do this, you'll make it work. He should know that."

"We'll see." I shove my coat and bag in the corner and get ready for the day. A stack of pink flyers catch my eye. "What's this?"

"Tell me you can read. I've been cheering you on to follow your dreams based on the assumption you're literate."

"Everyone's a comedian." It's a call out for amateur night. A bistro a few blocks down. I scan the announcement, then turn back to Alec. "What do you think of this?"

"I've been to it a few times; it's pretty good. The bistro's got good eats. They give you a free latte and muffin."

"Payment in service. I'm already a professional." I take the sheet and spend the rest of the day fretting how to get permission from Dad.

CHAPTER FOURTEEN

DUPLICITY IS MULTIFORKED

When the weekend comes, there's no way to avoid dinner at Uncle Raj's, so I go and hope he'll leave me alone. As soon as I step in the door, I know that's a fantasy. He's watching me, and the fevered light in his eyes reminds me of the tales Grandma tells of Ole Higue, a jumby who sucks the blood of children and babies.

I hook my arm through Farah's, and we run up the stairs. After she closes the door, I say, "I need your help," and take the flyer for the amateur night out of my pocket.

She reads it. "What do you want me to do? Sing backup?"

"Thanks"—I snatch the paper from her hand—"but I'm trying to win."

"You've never heard me sing."

"Can you?"

She leans back against the pillows and closes her eyes. "This is about you, not me."

"That's what I thought."

Her eyes pop open. "What do you want from me?"

"Help."

"No duh, ninny."

"I want to go to this."

"So? Go."

I explain Dad's ban on trumpet playing. "I can't even play in the house."

"Sic Grandma on him."

"She won't step in."

That makes her sit up. "She's not doing anything?"

I shake my head.

"Nothing at all?"

"What part of 'she's not doing anything' are you missing? Am I not enunciating properly?"

Her phone bings and she glances at it.

"You need to take it?"

"It's just Noah. I'll catch him later."

I don't think the words "just" and "Noah" will ever be together in any sentence I speak, but I shove down the jealousy by reminding myself that at this moment, she's choosing to be with me, not him. Instinct says these moments will be fewer and farther between, and I better enjoy them.

"Why isn't Grandma stepping in for you?"

"Trust me, I've begged, but she just smiles and pats my cheek."

"I hate it when she does that."

"Me too."

We sit, not talking, and I try to keep my thoughts away from why Noah's texting Farah and not me.

"She must want you to fix it. There's no way she agrees with him."

"No duh, ninny." It feels good to throw her words back, then less good when she launches a pillow at my face.

"So, fix it."

"If I could fix it, I would. That's why I'm here, talking to you."

"What do you want me to do?"

"Oh my god, we just had that conversation. I need your help. You managed to get me to go on the trip to Florida without your parents figuring out what was really going on, and you pocketed the cash your dad gave you at the hotel. If anyone can help me, it's you."

"I can't help. My way is lying."

"I know. Teach me, oh wise and venerable master."

She shakes her head. "I can lie to my parents. Who cares? But your parents—Nira—" Her voice softens. "Don't do that to them. Not them. They're . . . pure."

I open my mouth to argue, then realize to her they are

concentrated love and goodness. "Great. Now what? I want to go to this."

"Go. It's not like the event's at midnight."

"Yeah, but—" Grandma calls us for dinner. There's no time to tell Farah that Dad will ask where I'm going and what I'm doing, and once he finds out, he'll take away Georgia.

We head downstairs, and it's the usual garbage. Amazing food and ulcer-inducing conversation. Aunty Gul, who seems incapable of answering any question with a direct answer. Mom, her smile brittle as she feigns interest in the conversation. Me, Farah, and Grandma quietly eating, pretending we don't notice the tension, the rivalry so intense it takes the taste of the plait bread and chicken stew.

Uncle Raj and Dad are fighting over something stupid, two dogs pulling on a bone that no one wants to eat. Dad's winning, which means Uncle Raj pulls out his favorite weapon.

"How are the house renovations coming?"

Dad stutters into silence. DIY home renovations. A deception told long ago to explain away the cracks in the countertops, the peeling paint on the landing.

"You know how it is," says Dad. "Trying to find time between work and family. Some of those projects need a whole weekend, more, and where do I find the time? There's always something going on. And now with Nira putting down that blasted trumpet, it's even more work for me, trying to get her to catch up on all the schoolwork she missed."

"I didn't miss any schoolwork." I don't point out that Dad hasn't helped me with homework since I was in grade four.

"Your marks dropped," says Dad.

He flinches when Uncle Raj crows, "Oh, dropped? What happened? Can't do more than one thing at a time?"

"I do just fine, a two-percent drop is nothing—" I catch the hint when Mom shoves bread at me—shut up, Nira—and do as she telepathically suggests.

"Two percent?" Uncle Raj screws up his face. "That's the difference between those who make it"—he sweeps his hand around the house, using himself as an example—"and those who don't." He glances at Dad, smirks, then reaches for his rum.

"I'm still the smartest kid in my classes." Why am I falling into the black hole of their rivalry?

"So is Farah, and she plays soccer and tutors." Uncle Raj holds up his fingers. "Three things and she's still the best."

Dad takes a breath and launches the next volley, and it hits me, how stupid this is. How hypocritical they are. Fighting and more fighting, so caught up in the war, they don't even see the reality of the land for which they battle. Especially Dad. Talking about how things don't matter, and eating his stomach with envy for Uncle Raj's possessions.

I look at Farah. She says I shouldn't lie, that Mom and Dad are pure, but they're not. They're as sullied as her parents. I know the truth of Uncle Raj and Aunty Gul, but I'm not saying a word. Isn't a lie of omission as bad as a lie explicitly told? If I'm keeping the truth from my parents by staying silent, then what does it matter if I stay silent about the things that matter to me?

"Farah and I are going out tomorrow night," I tell the family. "Not exactly sure what we're getting up to, but I'll probably invite Mac and a couple of others."

"What do you mean you're not sure what you're doing?" asks Dad. "You make the plan, then you invite people."

I smile. "Knowing this group, we'll end up at a café somewhere drinking lattes and listening to whatever music's coming through the speaker." I make eye contact with Farah. "In fact, how's that for the plan? You okay eating some danish and drinking coffee?"

She nods, her gaze on me, watching, weighing.

My easy smile's back on Dad. "That's the plan. I'll be home by nine. Maybe Farah can sleep over?" It's a good question. While the adults argue the logistics of Farah sleeping over, and whether she should spend the whole weekend, my heart slows its racing pace.

I haven't lied, and technically, I've told the truth. I just haven't given them a detailed itinerary of the night's plan. But I'm on the razor's edge between a liar and a truth-teller. On one side is Grandma, who speaks her mind. On the other side are my uncle and father, liars for life. I'm in the middle, and one false move might cut me in two.

———◇———

The bistro is eclectic with a decorative style that leans on the French countryside. White-and-blue theme, clean lines, and mismatched chairs that somehow end up being harmonious. A glass enclosure at the front is lined with colorful pastries. I check my wallet and make sure I have enough to bring Grandma home something full of chocolate and frosting. But I'm hoping she'll show up. I trod lightly with her because I didn't know how she'd feel about my walking the razor's edge, and mentioned that if she was going to go for a walk, she might enjoy stopping in at the bistro for a drink. Then followed it with a look that was heavy on the hint.

Georgia is in my hand, and I grip the case handle a little tighter. I thread my way past the tables to where Alec, Farah, Noah, Emily, and McKenzie sit. "You didn't all have to be here," I tell them as I drag a chair in between Emily and McKenzie, and sit down.

McKenzie gives my outfit a once-over. "That's what you're wearing?"

I stand. "I should check in." The barista at the counter takes my name and signs me up. In return for playing, I get a free medium latte and a muffin. I thank her, but I don't eat or drink. Too nervous, and the milk will mess with my throat when it comes time to play.

I take the food and drink back to the group, let them split it how they want, and pretend not to be jealous when Emily and McKenzie share the latte. The night starts, and I war between excitement and anxiety.

Some of the people who get up are amateurs. Poets whose prose needed a little more time on the editing floor, singers whose voices crack. A couple of members in the crowd throw each other snotty looks, silently judging and laughing.

I'm not. It's hard to get up there, and talent is a subjective thing. Still, I'm glad some people suck at their artistry. It gives me hope I won't be the worst.

Then there are the amateurs who are a breath away from making it professionally. A singer who brings everyone to tears with her rendition of Dana Glover's "It Is You (I Have Loved)" and a slam poet who raises the roof with his hilarious take on walking the streets of New York.

Then it's my turn. I take a breath, remind myself I'm not as bad as the worst person, not as good as the best. And it's all okay. We all have our place at this event. I take the trumpet case to the front, say to the crowd, "Just give me a second," smile, and breathe in relief when they smile back. I set up the accompaniment playlist and Bluetooth it to the portable speaker.

Then I take Georgia from the case. He's sleek and golden, shining under the string of white lights, and glinting with excitement.

I take him in my hands, and it all feels right. So what if he's not a "real" trumpet? So what if he's a little dented in places? He's mine, and I'm his, and together we've made Grandma happy and Farah sigh, and maybe at the end of the day that'll be enough.

But right now, right now, it's the moment Mr. Nam talked about, and I'm not going to squander it. I've got thirty seconds before my heart slams its way out of my chest. I lift Georgia to my lips and blow, do a quick scale. Then I close my eyes and forget about the crowd. I listen to the heartbeat of Georgia—steady and calm—and he slows mine, too.

I take a breath and blow, and the note is pure starlight, rising to the heavens and taking my soul with it. The crowd's eclectic, as diverse as the mismatched chairs they fill. I take another breath and start in with the first bars of "Over the Rainbow." It's an easy pick because most people know the song. And it's an easy pick, because cheesy or not, it's got the sentiment we all connect with—a land where troubles don't exist, a place of ultimate peace and love.

A few bars to connect, then I'm song melding with "Somewhere Out There." The garage band mix is coming in, drums and guitar, adding layers, fueling me. Then—I don't know what happens—maybe it's the joy of my soul and my dreams and my reality meeting up at this crossroads, the euphoric high of setting myself free to do the thing I want—but I stop worrying about the crowd. I'm focused, not on their faces, not on their thoughts or their judgment; I'm focused on their emotions. For one manic second, it's as though I can hear and feel every heartbeat in the crowd, and we're all beating the same rhythm. It's a crescendo wave, slamming against the ocean rocks; it's the roar of the thunderstorm hurtling across the prairie. It's the big bang, it's comets and stars, galaxies and the Milky Way. It's life, it's rhythm, and it electrifies my molecules.

Another breath, another high note. My fingers are slip-sliding along the keys, rifling up and down, triplet notes, eighth notes, jumping octaves and worlds. And suddenly, I'm off the script of the music. Something in me is rising and taking over, and I'm connected with every heartbeat, telling them my fears and worries, my dreams and hopes. I'm painting the sky with my story. My life is in the melody, my existence is in the breaths between the notes.

I tell them about the fights with my parents, the insecurity with McKenzie and Emily, the sadness of Noah and Farah. The notes rise and fall, building on each other until it's not just a story I'm telling, it's an epic.

My time with Georgia, all the days and nights practicing, has given my internal clock military efficiency. I only have a minute left, it says. I use the time, take the audience down, but leave them high, pull them with my music from the sadness and longing. With my last note, I leave them with hope and the possibility of a happy ending.

I open my eyes as the playlist melts into silence. Blink and blink again. The café has more people in it now than before. They're crowded around the doors and backed into the corner.

And no one is moving. They're all staring.

For a sick minute, I think I've done it wrong. My panicked gaze searches, seeking the eyes of those I know. Before I can see them, the crowd moves. They erupt. Whooping and hollering. Clapping, cheering.

For me.

For Georgia.

And I realize the full truth of what Mr. Nam said. It never mattered about what Georgia looked like, no one would ever care because he is music, and so am I.

I'm crying so hard, I can't see my case or my phone. My blurred vision registers someone beside me. Noah pulls me into a hug and whispers, "I knew you could do it, Super Spy."

CHAPTER FIFTEEN

OPPORTUNITY COMES WITH HEART PADDLES

I fall into an easy pattern with my family, and it only takes a couple of "We'll probably just hang out at a restaurant or something," for Dad to decide it's the regular thing with my friends and me. Part of it is the magical effect of having a job and keeping up my marks. Part of it is because Farah's always around, and he figures there's no way I'm getting into trouble if she's with me. I'm glad Dad's willing to loosen up. But a lot of it is Grandma.

I hadn't seen her at the bistro, but when I got home that night, she said, "I always loved 'Over the Rainbow.'" Since then, she's been on Dad to let me go out more, and he's listening. But his permission always comes at a cost, just like tonight, and it's always some kind of lecture or commentary on how I'm not reaching my potential.

"Doing nothing but sitting around, drinking expensive drinks and eating food you can get at home." He shakes his head. "Your kind has no direction."

"Raul, please." Mom turns from the stove where the hassa curry simmers. "We used to stand under the awning of Fogarty's, liming until the rain stopped."

"I wasn't liming," says Dad. "I was window shopping."

Mom looks at me and rolls her eyes.

Dad tries a few more half-hearted volleys, but he doesn't really care about what we're doing. My marks are up, thanks to a couple of extra-credit papers. At the last family dinner, I was ahead of Farah, so he's benevolent.

I'm drowning in ecstasy. I have to be careful not to do too many talent nights or amateur callouts. Going out during the weekend is one thing, but if I push too hard, Dad will get suspicious. It takes everything not to ask for permission, though. Playing is a drug, and I'm addicted.

Not every gig has been as great as the one at the bistro, and not every crowd has cheered like they did. Some of the people have been hostile, but there's always one person who appreciates what I did, and I focus on them. Besides, every time I play, I connect with Georgia, to the iridescent part of myself, and the music. It doesn't even matter that other than the latte and muffin, I haven't received any kind of payment for my playing.

I'm playing. I'm under the lights, Georgia wailing to a willing crowd, and for now, that's all the payment I need. More than that, I need the joy, the euphoria. Emily's pulling away. I know it, feel it, see it.

She won't meet my eyes when we talk. McKenzie doesn't even try to have a conversation with me anymore. They're a world of two, a coupe sedan with no seating for a third. I tell my sorrows to Georgia, and we share our pain with the crowds. The audience gives back, and by the end of each night, I walk away taller and stronger.

I'm at Reynolds, closing out the cash register for the night when a guy comes in just as Alec's going to lock the door. "We're a minute from the end of the night," he tells the man.

"I'll just be a second, promise." He smiles and leans on the door.

Alec sighs but steps back, and shoots me a look that's a combination of exasperation and apology.

"Nira?" The man comes over.

"Uh, yeah." I shut the cash drawer and tuck the money under the counter.

"Jerry Caplan." He holds out his hand. "I was at the café—Brockman's—the other night, and I heard you play. You were fabulous."

"Oh, thanks." I shake his hand.

Alec gives me a wink, and a thumbs-up from behind Jerry's back.

"I was wondering"—Jerry reaches into his blazer and pulls out a business card—"I own the Ambassador Hotel. It's down on—"

"I know where it is." Glass and metal, mixed with stone and wood. It's the go-to place for celebrities and dignitaries.

He holds the card, and I take it. "I wonder if I might talk to you about performing in our restaurant."

"You want me to play at your hotel?" I'm an idiot, repeating his words, but I can't believe what I'm hearing.

He nods. "Maybe we can work out a schedule with your other job and school." Jerry smiles at Alec, who smiles back.

"Uh, sure, I'd like that," I say.

"There's a catch."

Of course, there is.

"I want you to be exclusive to the hotel."

I frown. "So, no more playing amateur nights or talent shows?"

"No, no, that's fine. I just don't want you to play at another restaurant." He takes a fast breath. "You have a gift, something special. I think you would help boost patronage."

My head feels like someone has tossed it in the heavy load cycle of a washing machine, and I'm struggling to stay upright. He thinks I can bring people in. He thinks I'll be good for business.

"If you're here, they'll come back."

"But you have celebrities staying at your hotel." Holy crap. I could play in front of someone famous. "Do you really need me?"

Jerry's mouth screws to the side. "The famous crowd can be flaky. My hotel one day, next day, it's someone else they love. But you, your music, you would bring people in."

I nod, too stunned to do anything else.

"You'll have to sign a contract—"

"A contract?" The good feeling evaporates into the air. I'm not eighteen, which means I have to have a parent sign for me. And neither will.

Jerry nods.

I don't want to turn down the chance, but I can't tell him I'm playing on the sly. "Before we talk about contracts and exclusivity, I think I'd like to come and visit, maybe do a gig and see how I feel."

"That's fair." He points at his card. "Check your schedule and let me know?"

"Done."

"We should grab a pic." Alec pulls out his phone. "Nira's first big break."

We smile for the camera, and Jerry leaves. When he's gone, Alec locks the door. "Smart, delaying him."

"What?"

"It could be a con." He holds up his hands. "I hope not, but he could have sneaked into the hotel office, taken a bunch of business cards. It happens all the time in doctors' offices."

The good feeling's turned to salt, and it's corroding me.

"Nira." Alec snaps his fingers. "Chill. That's why I took the picture." He airdrops it to my phone. "Go to the hotel, ask around, and find out if he's legit. If he is, then play your session, see how you feel. If it's good, sign the contract."

"You don't understand." I tell him about my dad.

"Tell him."

"You're kidding. Why didn't I think of that? I'll tell him, he'll be thrilled, and the contract is signed." I hand Alec the night's cash out. "He's going to freak."

"Nira, I saw you at the bistro. This is what you love."

"He's not going to care."

"But you should. You should care enough, love the music and Georgia enough to step into the fray, and face the freak-outs."

I think about what Alec says as I get on the bus and head to the Ambassador. He's right, but I still want to deny his truth. My dad will freak, and freak hard. I could lose Georgia. If I keep going the way I have, playing in the dark and the shadows, I can keep going until I'm strong enough to take on my father. But Jerry's offer dangles, sparkling starlight I can almost touch.

I text Emily and ask if she has time to talk.

NOT FEELING SO GOOD. MAYBE LATER?

I send her a happy face and tell her I'll try again, in a bit. The bus halts at my stop, and I head down the street to the hotel. A gray-suited doorman tips his hat and opens one of the glass doors for me. I scan the walls and decor for a picture of Jerry but don't see one. Hoping Alec is wrong, hoping he's right, I move to the front desk.

"Can I help you?" The man behind the counter smiles, and his accent makes me think of savannahs, elephants, and rhinos.

"Hi, uh, I have a weird question." I open my phone and show him the picture of Jerry and me. "Do you know him?"

He grins. "Jerry's the owner."

"Oh." I breathe out the tension. "Thanks."

"You took a photo with a stranger?" Curiosity plays in his words.

"Yes—no—he came to my work, asked me if I would play at the restaurant—"

His grin widens. "Oh, the trumpet girl."

"What?"

"I bartend when we're short-staffed." He glances around, then pulls a biology textbook from under the counter. "I need all the hours I can get to pay for school. When I was on shift last week, Jerry told me about you."

We talk for a bit, and I get an idea of Jerry as a boss. Fair but tough, generous but exacting. I could live with that. When we're done, I thank him, then head to the restaurant. I want to take a look, see what the stage might look like. The doors to the restaurant are dark wood with long golden handles. I imagine the inside looks like a forties snapshot, large, circular booths where couples can get lost in each other. Or maybe it's oiled walnut counters at the bar and Tiffany lamps in the middle of the tables.

My heart stutters when Noah comes out the exit. I smile, move faster, but he's got his head down, and he doesn't see me. He turns and heads back inside. I stop, unsure of what it is about his posture that tells me to hang back.

He comes out a few seconds later, but he's not alone. He's got his arm around a guy, supporting him as they walk. The guy is an older version of him. He leans on Noah, says something to him. Noah doesn't respond, and his face is empty of emotion.

The restaurant is forgotten. I trail behind them. Then I stop. Maybe this is wrong. If I was supposed to know any of this, Noah would've told me. This secret he's carried alone. Who am I to take it from him? Just as I decide to step back, Noah's dad stumbles and goes down. I run, grab him before he falls, and hurt both of them.

"Thanks, but I got this." Noah's focus turns from his dad to me. His eyes widen when he realizes the person on the other side isn't a stranger, but me.

"Let's get him in the car," I say before he can dismiss me, and I start moving before he can argue.

"The underground garage." They're the only words Noah speaks during the ordeal to get his father across the lobby and down the corridor. Common sense says it only takes us a couple of minutes, but the quiet humiliation of Noah, the drunken obliviousness of his dad, and the stares of the strangers along our path make it feel like an eternity.

We go to the elevator and ride it down. His dad hums a tune without melody and smiles my way. I don't look at Noah, but my peripheral says he doesn't do anything but stare straight ahead.

The doors open and Noah leads us through the maze of cars to a silver SUV. It chirps open.

"Do you want him in the back seat?" I ask.

"I need him in the front." He's still not looking at me. "In case he starts vomiting."

There's no good response to that.

Noah opens the door, and we pour his dad into the front passenger.

"I'll make it up to you." His dad tries to put his hand on Noah's shoulder, misses, tries again, and again, then makes contact the fourth time. "Acapulco."

"We've been."

"Costa Rico." He slurs the words, rolls the *r*, and gives me a fuzzy smile.

"Costa *Rica*. That was last year."

"We'll figure it out." He burps and grins like a well-fed baby as Noah belts him in. The door clicks shut, and the SUV chirps as Noah locks in his dad.

Noah traces the handle with his finger. "Don't tell anyone. Don't—"

I grip his fingers. "I won't."

"He's not always like this."

"Why didn't you tell me?"

"You're kidding, right?" He flashes me a smile in the window's reflection. "Open up to the Super Spy? It took forever to find out you played the trumpet. Telling you about my dad—"

"I'm sorry." I squeeze his hand. "I was ashamed." It all feels so stupid and trivial now.

"Me too." He threads his fingers through mine.

Memory spins, thinking of how often Noah goes away with his dad, putting together his dad's offer for another trip. "Three times a year, or so, your dad . . . has a moment?"

"I never know when it's going to happen. Everything's fine, and it's fine, then he's gone for a day, maybe two. The good moments are like today when he's still sober enough to call me." The words sound heavy, and Noah's exhaustion is a physical thing I can touch.

He looks my way. It's not like I'm seeing him for the first time, but there's a layer and a texture to him that I've never noticed. The faint lines around his eyes, the tiredness that rims his mouth. And I feel like such a schmuck. He's hurting, tired, embarrassed, and I want to be a good friend and comfort him. But I also want to dive into him, into all the layers and lines that make him, him.

"We're in therapy. It's not all bad."

I squeeze his fingers. "You're still better off than me. My parents will have me in therapy till I die."

He smiles, grateful for the understanding. "I'm sure it's not that bad."

"My dad doesn't believe in therapy, so I'll have to wait until he's dead. In the meantime, I comfort myself by imagining the nursing homes I'll put them in. You'd be amazed how cathartic it can be."

"You got visions of Nurse Ratched?" He grins.

"More like an overly sympathetic, caring nurse who constantly asks him how he's feeling, forces him into therapy, and spoon-feeds him Jell-O. The green kind. He hates the green kind."

Noah laughs. "Super Spy. I should have figured there was a dark side to you."

Our gazes drift to his father. His hands are up, and he seems to be conducting an orchestra only he can hear.

"He doesn't seem to be an angry drunk." I don't know what else to do, and I don't want to leave Noah like this.

"Mom died—that's when it started. When he misses her too

much, he drinks. He says she comes to him when he's drunk."

"Do you believe him?"

Noah blinks fast. "I still dream about her." He glances at me and smiles as though he's talking too much but can't stop himself. "She loved to travel."

"The holidays are his way of saying sorry, aren't they?"

"His way of saying sorry," Noah repeats. "Yeah, they are, not that his sorries mean much, anymore." He tosses me another faint smile.

"I'm sorry." I regret the words as soon as they're out of my mouth.

Noah turns toward me. "You are, aren't you?"

I shrug, not trusting myself to speak.

Something changes in the way he's holding my hand. Maybe it's the soft turn so our palms meet, maybe it's the way he's twined his fingers in mine. "You really are the sweetest person I know."

Then he's kissing me. Kissing me. Kissing me. I'm lost in the scent and feel of him, lost in the taste of my first kiss.

The bang of the glass wrenches me away. His dad taps the glass again, grins, and gives us both a thumbs-up. Noah sighs and shakes his head.

I touch my lips. They tingle from the kiss; they feel seared by his touch.

Noah catches my movement. "Did I hurt you?"

I shake my head. "No, I—" I don't know what to say, don't want to say the wrong thing. But when panic and worry tinge Noah's eyes, I blurt out, "I really liked it."

He grins with relief. "Me too."

"But should I have done this?"

"Kiss me? Yes. You should've. You should keep doing it." He puts his hands on my hips and moves me back, away from his dad.

"But you're in an emotional—this, your dad—am I taking advantage of you?"

His laughter echoes along the cement walls. He traces the point where my hair and forehead meet, tracing the line to my ear, and my skin lights up.

"How sweet can you possibly be?" He leans in and kisses me, again.

I'm drowning, I'm flying. I'm rooted so deep into the earth, I feel the heat of its core on my feet. I'm unanchored, floating among the stars and comets. Noah is music, he's a melody I don't want to stop playing.

Deep in the recess of my brain, I hear the ping. Farah. And I pull away. "Noah—" I tremble and give myself to the moment when he touches my lips. Then I take his hand. "Farah."

His eyebrows pull together. "What about Farah?"

"She likes you—and you like her—"

He stares at me for a too-long second, then his eyes go wide, and he laughs. "Yeah, I like Farah, and Farah likes me, but we don't like each other like that." His head tilts to the side. "It's always been you, Nira. Didn't you know that?"

I shake my head.

"That's what Farah said," he murmurs. "She said to be patient with you because, for all your smarts, you can be a—" He stops.

I fill in the blank. "A ninny?"

"Moronic ninny were her exact words."

"Yeah, that's Farah." God, I'm such an idiot. She must have known Noah liked me, must have known the whole time, and I was the moron who went off on her because I was jealous. "I really am a ninny." I press my forehead into the welcome strength of his chest. "You were spending so much time together, texting, and—"

"And you thought I liked her."

I look up, and his eyes are full of smoke and fire.

"And the whole time you liked me."

I nod and take a breath. "Yes, I like you, very much."

He smiles, then twitches and looks at the passenger side, his energy that of a parent who knows every sound their baby makes. "I should go."

"Do you want me to come with you? Do you need help?"

He presses his mouth to mine and murmurs, "Nira. So sweet, so good." Noah pulls away. "No, I'm good. Dad and I have a rhythm." He tilts his head. "Why are you here? At the hotel?"

"Oh! We'll talk later." I back away before the temptation to throw myself into his arms and feel the heat of him overwhelms me. "We'll talk later, promise."

"Do you need a ride home?"

"I have to do something here."

"What?"

"I'll tell you later."

"Okay, Super Spy, keep your secrets. I'll text you later." He comes toward me. "Come on, I'll walk you back to the elevator."

"What about your dad?"

He peers into the window. "He'll be fine for a couple of minutes." Noah holds out his hand.

I smile and take it.

CHAPTER SIXTEEN

REJECTION IS A VELVET COAT

I get off the elevator, but I'm too wound up to go to the restaurant. I want to talk to Farah, but I feel like a grade-A moron for the stupid fight, and I need time to figure out how to start our conversation. Emily lives a couple of blocks from here. I text her to see if she's around. No answer. Maybe she's not around; maybe she's misplaced her phone again. Maybe she doesn't want to answer me.

I debate for a second. No, it can't be the last one. Things have been decent between us. Maybe it's time for us to stop being decent to each other and start being best friends again. I text my mom and tell her I'm going to Emily's house.

A couple of seconds later, she replies, saying to let her know if I need a ride home.

I tuck my phone in my pocket and head out. The entire walk, I'm lost in the change between Noah and me. Lost in the cluelessness of his feelings to me, lost in the multihued prism of what might be with us.

The doorman at Emily's building smiles at me in recognition and opens the door. I smile back and go inside, my ears and face grateful for the warmth. The concierge knows me, too. "Good evening, miss. Chilly out tonight, isn't it?" he says as he swivels the sign-in book my way.

We chat for a second. I ask about his dog, and he tells me all is well. I hand the pen back to him, then take the elevator to Emily's floor. Excitement is bubbling inside me. Yeah, we've been distant, and yeah, she's been odd, but this is Emily and me. This is Noah and me. She's going to want to hear about it, including the news about Jerry's job offer.

I knock on the door and wait.

Noise on the other side, then the door swings open to McKenzie's voice, "You better watch yourself, because I'm coming for you." There's a teasing note in her words, and Emily's laughter follows.

McKenzie steps out from behind the door, her focus on the money in her hand. "I think this is what we owe you—" She looks up. The happiness in her face shatters into horror as she sees me. "Nira." My name is a mangled syllable on her mouth. "What are you doing here?"

I'm irritated at the suggestion I don't belong. The accusatory tone of her voice inflames me. My memory adds fire, as well. In the back of my mind is Emily's text about not feeling good. She didn't have time for me, but she had it for McKenzie. "Emily's my friend—" What a lie.

"What's going on?" Emily's words are distant and growing closer. "Can't you do the math, Mac?" She opens the door even wider, sees me. Her expression mirrors McKenzie's horror. "Oh. Um—" She and McKenzie exchange a miserable look. "What are you doing here?"

I don't have an answer. My last words were "Emily's my friend," but everything in her posture, her words, her expression says the opposite. "Uh, nothing, never mind."

She forces a fake smile, and my heart shatters. "Come on in. We were waiting for the pizza delivery." A brittle laugh follows. "But you're sure no pizza guy."

"I'm good. Uh, have a good night. We'll talk later." I turn, flee for the elevator, and leave the confetti of my broken heart scattering in my wake.

CHAPTER SEVENTEEN

HOSTILITY HAS QUILLS

I run up the stairs and into the house.

Mom finds me as I'm hanging my coat up. "Home so early? I thought you'd want me to pick you up."

I stare at the threads on my coat, trying to get a grip on the high-low of the past few hours. I'm trying to figure out if we only get so much happiness in the world, and once we reach that level, the gods pull us back by taking away some of the things we love most.

"Nira?"

I try to hide it, and I try to hide it, but my shoulders start shaking, and suddenly, I'm sobbing into my jacket.

Mom grabs me and turns me around, into her embrace. "Shh, shh." She smooths my hair. "It's okay."

I can't find words; I just keep crying on her shoulder. We stand like that until I have no more tears left. When I pull away from her, babbling an apology about the giant wet spot on her shoulder, I see Grandma standing to the side.

"I've made tea. You come and tell me all about it." She gives Mom the eye.

Mom's lips press together, then she nods, smiles, kisses me, and moves away.

I shake my head. "I don't want to talk about it, not yet."

"Come. The tea is getting cold." Grandma takes me by the hand and leads me into the kitchen. "Are you hungry?"

"No, I don't want to eat anything."

"Okay, I'll get you some meat pie and cheese straw."

"I don't want to eat."

"You just cried out your body weight."

"I'm not hungry."

"You will be."

"Later." I sit down. "But not yet."

"Okay, okay." She holds up her hands. "Just the cheese straws." She fixes the tea and gives it to me.

I take a sip. "There's hardly any sugar. Doesn't that violate some cardinal rule about sugar in tea solving all the problems."

"Sugar doesn't solve problems. Sugar is there to help with the shock and helps steel you for the strength you need to tackle the problem. The more sugar, the more power you need."

"Just a bit of sugar because—?"

"I don't know what happened. Until I know, I can't give you sugar." She sits beside me. "What's going on?"

"I don't even know where to start."

She looks over her shoulder, then leans in. "Is it about Georgia and the playing?"

I shake my head.

"Okay." She pats my knee. "I wanted to ask before I let Safiya into the kitchen." She takes my cup, rises, and calls for my mom.

"What is it? What happened?"

And it comes pouring out. Emily, McKenzie, the breakup of the friendship. Through it all, Mom rubs my shoulders, Grandma hands me tissues, and I drink the tea. I reach for more sugar, but Grandma pushes my hand away. "You don't need it."

When it's all over, I go to my room. I'm wrung out. There's no energy to give to Georgia. I check my phone. Nothing from Emily or Mac. I text Noah but don't get anything in return. Farah would text back, but I still don't know how to talk to her about Noah. I'm alone in my misery and regret, and not even the happiness of Noah and me is enough to dispel the darkness.

I cover my head with my pillow and lie, star-shaped, on the bed. I'm not sure how long I'm there, unmoving, when the door slams open. I jerk upright, the pillow falling from my face.

Farah stands in the doorway. "You're such a ninny. Your life is falling apart, and you can't text? I have to hear about it from Grandma?"

I crumple, she swears, slams the door, and runs to me. "What happened?"

"I'm so sorry. I'm so stupid."

"Don't apologize for that. I've always known you're stupid."

I laugh through my tears and punch her shoulder. "Shouldn't you be at home getting another A so Uncle Raj can gloat?"

She rolls her eyes. "Him. I told them I'm sleeping over."

"On a school night? They let you?"

"What're they going to do? I'm with family."

I take her hand. "Thanks. Thanks for coming over."

"Grandma's too old to deal with your nonsense." She smiles as she speaks. "What are you sorry for?"

"I'm apologizing for Noah."

"You already did."

I tell her about what happened in the hotel, but I don't tell her about his dad. My reason for being there is the job offer, and I say I just happened to run into Noah.

"Oh my god, you had someone ask you to play? As a job? Nira!" She hugs me hard.

I pry myself from her. We'll talk about that later." Then I tell her about the kiss, and the other kiss, and the other kiss.

"I'm still lost. Why are you apologizing?"

"Because I was jealous and stupid—"

"Right, and you said sorry."

"But the whole time you knew he liked me, and you never told."

Farah looks at me like I'm a moron. "It wasn't my secret to tell."

"I know, and that's what makes it even worse. You were honoring Noah, and I acted like such a—"

"Ninny?"

"Moronic ninny." I take her hand. "Thanks for being a good friend to him, and to me. It would have been easy to get mad and—"

"I don't tell secrets." She holds my gaze. "Neither do you. So, come on, out with it. What made you cry?"

She spends the night, and we talk about Emily and McKenzie until there's no more talking to be done. Farah's convinced something else is going on. "Emily loves you. No way would she dump you like that."

"But McKenzie—"

"—is odd, sure, and for sure she has an agenda, but I don't think she was looking to mess you up with Emily." She cocks her head. "Do you think they're dating?"

"No way. Don't you ever see McKenzie with Noah? She's one touch away from rubbing a hole in his arm."

"Maybe she's bi."

I consider it, then shake my head. "No. No way. If Emily liked McKenzie, she'd tell me."

"Because you've been such a good friend to both of them."

"Why do I have to defend myself? McKenzie's as racist as a Confederate general."

"No, she's not. I'm telling you, Nira, there's something else going on."

We keep talking, keep debating. I lend her some of my clothes.

We're lying side by side in bed, sleep creeping in, when I say, "Farah?"

"Yeah?"

"That day we saw—the time in Florida with your dad—I asked you about how his choices would affect you—"

She laughs softly. "Yeah, you and your mother hen routine about my long-term growth and development."

"You said you had a plan, and I thought you meant Noah."

She doesn't say anything.

"So?" I ask into the silence. "What's your plan?"

"You won't laugh?"

"Should I?"

She shifts closer, and even though the room is dark, she finds my hand and holds it. "Mom and Dad want me to be a doctor, and I will be. What they don't know is that my patients will be creatures—not humans." She squeezes my fingers. "I want to be a veterinarian." She says the words with the same yearning I have when I talk about being a musician. "When I'm established in my practice, I'm going to buy a house, somewhere in the country, close enough for me to commute"—she takes a breath—"and then I'm going to rescue as many animals as I can." The mattress bends as she turns, and I sense the glow in her eyes. "I can see it, Nira. I can *feel* it. A house with lots of windows and hardwood floors. And every morning, I'll hear the *click-click* of my dogs' and cats' feet, and the sound of a cat purring on my lap, the *thump* of the dogs' tails on the floor."

"King-size bed," I say after a minute.

"What?"

"You should have a king-size bed so you can dream together. You won't hear their footsteps in the morning because they'll be with you, but—"

She throws her arms around me and hugs me tight.

We talk about her dream, how much her parents will freak out because they don't like animals and a vet doesn't have the same status—in their minds—as a surgeon. Farah falls asleep in the middle of telling me how her house will smell of lemon wood oil and fresh bread. It's early in the morning when my phone buzzes. Noah.

SORRY. His apology lights up my screen. FELL ASLEEP. GUESS I WAS MORE TIRED THAN I THOUGHT.

NO WORRIES. YOU OKAY?

:-)

COOL.

Y WERE YOU AT THE HOTEL?

LONG STORY. TELL YOU LATER.

SUPER SPY STRIKES AGAIN.

I'm giddy. This thing between us is precious. It ripples in my heart like sunlight on the ocean, and I want to float in it. We text nothing, happy faces, and stupid memes, but god, it's me, and it's Noah, and I'm going to hold on to it for as long as I can.

When I wake up, it's because Mom is rubbing my shoulder. "I told the school you're not coming in today. I thought you could use the day off."

"What did Dad say?"

"Your marks are good; he's fine."

Something in the way she says it makes me think she went Momma Bear on him, but I don't say anything. I sit up, shaking the sleep from my brain. "Thanks." My cousin was right. In their way, my parents have their purity. "Where's Farah?"

Mom sucks her teeth. "Raj, what else? I tried to get him to let the poor girl stay with you, but he's convinced it's some conspiracy. I want her to fail in school so your marks will be higher." She pushes off the bed. "Honestly, your father and his brother. Sometimes I want to throw them off a cliff."

"Don't. They'd just argue about who's falling faster."

She laughs, kisses me, then leaves to get ready for work. I text

Farah and tell her thanks. She texts me back an emoji of a middle finger. Then I text Noah, tell him I won't be around today, but I should be at work tonight if he wants to stop by. I pull the covers over me and go back to bed.

When I wake up, it's just Grandma and me in the house. I grab breakfast and a shower, then head outside with her when she suggests we go for a walk. She takes me on one of her many routes, past the elementary school and playground, through the park where the old men play chess while dressed in woolen caps and parkas. The smoke rises from their pipes and scents the air with tobacco and cherry.

Grandma doesn't talk, except to point out the birds on the branches or a brittle leaf swirling in the breeze. I'm happy for the silence. My thoughts veer between the trumpet and Noah, Emily and Farah's theories. We turn a corner and another corner and come to a dead end.

"Oh." Grandma pivots. "I didn't realize they'd shut down the road."

I take in the men working on the other side of the orange barricades. "Sewer work."

"What a waste. I thought the path would be clear."

"Let's turn around and find some other way. Anyway, it's not a loss; it was a nice walk."

"Hmm, if you say so."

I catch the light in her eye, the tilt of her mouth, and stop walking. "You've got to be kidding me."

"What?"

"Did you take me on this winding path to teach me something?"

"We should go home. The cold is poking your brain full of holes. You don't make sense."

"Oh, please. You're as subtle as a . . . as a . . ."

"See? Holes in the brain." She starts down the path.

I chase after her. "Come on, admit it. This was a learning exercise. Take me down some winding path, give me a dead end, and I'm supposed to put it all together as a metaphor for my friendship with Emily. Right? It wasn't a waste because there were good things that came of the relationship, just like how we saw the birds and the old men."

"I didn't say a word, but it was nice to see those things. You're right; it wasn't a waste."

"Old woman—"

"And since you're waxing philosophical, then you're right. No path is a dead end. We're meant to walk around, get lost, and go the wrong way down the one-way street."

I put my arm around her shoulder. "Well played, Yoda. When we get home, I'll make you some tea."

But when we get home, McKenzie is standing on the steps.

CHAPTER EIGHTEEN

REVELATION IS
A POINTED OBJECT

"You must be cold." Grandma's words break the tense silence. "Come inside. I'll make you tea."

I pull Grandma into me. "You shouldn't have done that. This isn't a road we need to travel. She's a dead end on so many levels."

"Good you know that," she replies. "You won't be surprised."

"Old woman—"

"Enjoy the birds." She smiles at McKenzie. "How long have you been waiting?"

"Not that long," she says, but her cheeks are wind-bitten and her fingers are the color of raw meat.

We get into the house, and I'm forced to be polite. "Can I hang up your coat?" All I want to do is strangle her with it.

"No, I'm fine." She pulls the sleeves over her fingers.

"Come into the kitchen," says Grandma. "I'll make you some tea."

"I'm not staying"—she gestures to me—"I came to talk to Nira. I'll be quick."

Grandma nods. "Maybe some other time." She leaves.

McKenzie shifts her weight, her gaze ping-ponging around the room.

I'm frozen with anger and the added violation of having her in my house. "So?"

She jerks her head. "Yeah—um—"

She's shaking. "Come away from the door if you're cold." Ever the hostess, even when I want to throttle her.

"It's all my fault," she blurts out. "What's going on between you and Emily. That's on me."

"Tell me something I don't know."

She flinches.

"If that's all you came to say—"

"I'm sorry—" She hiccups and starts crying.

I'm lost. I have no idea if her tears are real or not. If they are, I'm out of my depth. What am I supposed to do with a despondent McKenzie?

Someone raps me on the back of my head. I turn and find myself under Grandma's glare. She holds out a box of tissues and waves them at McKenzie. I take them, and Grandma moves back down the hall.

"Here." I hold out the box.

"Thanks." McKenzie helps herself to a couple and wipes her face. "This is harder than I thought."

I still think she might be faking it, but common sense says McKenzie doesn't have the smarts to act this well. Now I'm disconcerted because her crying makes her more human, and I don't know what to do with this new facet of her personality.

"It's my fault." She snuffles into the tissue. "When it all started happening, Emily wanted to be up front and tell you, but I told her not to say anything." She crumples the sodden wads and shoves them in her pocket.

I hand her another tissue.

"I was scared of how you'd react."

"No kidding. How did you think I'd react?" Poor choice of words. She starts crying, again. I'm trying to stay sympathetic, but she's stolen my friend, and now she wants me to forgive her for it.

If I don't shut her up, her wailing will get Grandma back here, and I'm not set for another whack on the head. I pat McKenzie on the shoulder. "It's—stop crying."

"I can't," she wails. "I'm so scared of you."

My hand freezes in midair. "What?"

But she's in full babble mode. "You're intimidating."

What?

"When it started happening, Emily wanted to be honest and tell you. She was all 'Nira's my best friend,' but I know you can't stand me, so I told her to wait, and we'd see, but then things got worse and—" She sobs into her tissue.

"What are you talking about?"

"The first time I saw you, you were so different, so together."

I still don't know what she's talking about. "Take off your coat, and we'll get you some tea."

"No, I can't—I want to be honest with you, to make amends. I have to start from the beginning, from the first time I saw you, and how scared I was."

One of the most popular girls in school, frightened of the immigrant girl with the tuna fish sandwich. "You should sit; you're obviously suffering side effects of dehydration from all the crying."

"I'm serious, Nira. I want to be your friend." She sniffs. "But it went wrong. It always goes wrong with you. I try, and I try, but every time I'm around you, you give me that look, and I get intimidated and say stupid things."

I don't even know what to say. The way I'm looking at her must be The Look because she says, "See? I'm pouring out my soul, and you're just staring."

"I'm sorry. It's just—every time you talk to me, you just come off—"

"Racist and ignorant? I know. Every time—every time—I sound like I should be burning a cross or something. I know you're not Hindi, I know what halal meat is, I know you're not anorexic." Her words pick up speed. "I'm trying to impress you with how culturally savvy I am, and it comes out wrong every time. Then I try to make a joke about it because humor is supposed to bond people together, and it goes horrifically sideways. The harder I try, the worse it gets. I'm babbling like a moron, and I can hear the voice inside my head screaming *shut up*, *shut up*, but I can't. I keep going." She reaches for another tissue. "And the thing is, I'm not, I swear I'm not racist. I'm a really good person. I'm kind and sometimes funny. I like it when it rains, and I love animals, and"—she watches me like it's her last breath and I need to hear her words—"I'm not stupid."

No, but maybe I am.

"When it all started going down with Emily, she was so excited, and she wanted to tell you, but I said go slow. You didn't like me, baby steps, right?"

"Uh, I guess."

"Emily told you to call me Mac, not McKenzie, but you wouldn't. You only give your nicknames to your friends, and that's something we'll never be."

The light that's in her goes out. I've hurt her, and the realization takes the light out of me. Tell me I haven't been running around, wounding her the same way she's wounded me.

"You don't like me, and I get that, but I really like Emily, and I'm good for her, I promise."

"I get you like Emily, but—" And then it hits. I'm an idiot. Jeez! I'm an idiot. "You're dating Emily."

She nods, miserable. "Emie wanted to tell you, but—"

"I didn't realize you—I thought you liked Noah. You're always touching him, sitting beside him. You don't—I would never have guessed you like girls." Farah will never let me forget she was right about this.

"It's . . . easier for kids not to know about"—she waves her hands—"this. Me. I know how to put on a good show."

I tug her coat, and she slips it from her shoulders. Grandma magically appears. "The tea is ready. I put out jam cookies and tartlets."

"Thank you," says McKenzie, "but I'm not hungry or thirsty."

"Just the cookies, then," says Grandma, then vanishes like an apparition.

McKenzie puts her shoes by the door and follows me into the kitchen. The mugs, milk, and sugar sit beside the teapot, and a circle of jam cookies is tucked to the side.

"My family doesn't know. None of the kids at school, either. Most of them wouldn't care, I guess. Noah for sure wouldn't care. But my parents—they would—" She shudders. "It never mattered because there wasn't really anybody for a long time. But then there was Emie—" She sighs. "She's something else entirely."

I pour her a cup of tea. "You said it."

We share a smile.

"Do you take milk or sugar?"

McKenzie's nose wrinkles. "I'm not sure. I've never had tea."

"Sugar and milk. You always have that in times of distress and sadness." I fix her tea and hand her a cookie. "I'm sorry you didn't think you could tell anyone. You could have told me."

"That's what Emie said, but how do you share a secret with someone who can't stand you?"

I wince. "I'm sorry. Emily told me I wasn't giving you a chance, but I was so caught up in losing her—"

"You can't ever lose her. She loves you to the sky and back."

Her words should make me feel better, but I feel worse. "I should've trusted our friendship."

"I love watching the two of you." McKenzie takes a sip of the tea and smiles as the taste hits her tongue. "You guys are a real friendship, you know? I don't have that. No one at school knows the true me. I'm invisible. You wouldn't know what it feels like, but it sucks."

I want to laugh. I want to cry. The most popular girl at my school is sitting at my table and telling me no one sees her. Shame heats my cheeks. "I thought you were taking my place as her friend.

I didn't realize she was in love and in a relationship."

McKenzie sets down her tea. "I could never take your place."

"If I'd known—I'm sorry. I'm sorry I was so caught up in my own damage, I couldn't see the truth of you."

"It's not your fault. I sound like a fascist every time I talk to you."

"But now we know, right? You sound slightly off when you talk to me; that's okay. I'm used to quirky people. Look at Emily. She always drops her sentences and waits for me to finish them off."

"You caught that, too?" Mac laughs. "It drives me crazy. Like, just say it, okay? Finish the thought!"

"I'm glad you're together. If you make her happy, then I'm glad you're together."

Tears fill her eyes. "We're not," she whispers. "Not anymore. She was so mad at me last night. It's been tearing her apart, not being able to tell you about us. She's such an honest person."

"But she'd never tell someone else's secret. She tried to tell me to stop being such a judgmental idiot and give you a chance, but I was too busy being a judgmental idiot to hear her."

"The look on your face when you came to the house—" She lifts her hand, as if to reach for me, then lets it fall back. "I never meant to hurt you. But I was scared, and now Emie—" She pushes the mug away. "She never liked being quiet about the relationship, and she thinks you're mad at her for not sharing. And now she's mad at me for, well, everything. She broke up with me. I've messed up everything."

"No, or at least, it's not all you. I'm sorry. This is on me." I take her hand. "Finish your tea. We'll fix this, okay? We'll go and talk to Emily."

"Thanks." She wipes the tears from her eyes. "Thanks for giving me a second chance."

"Me too. Thanks, Mac."

CHAPTER NINETEEN

BRAVERY IS A RED FLAG

I t takes thirty seconds to fix the rift between Emily and Mac, five minutes for Emily to lecture me on being insecure in our friendship, and two hours of pizza, movies, and laughter to make everything right in the world.

I make my way home, my head ringing with everything that's happened in the past forty-eight hours. The essence of it all sticks with me. I know what I have to do, and it's a risk that will either win me everything or it's a gamble where I lose it all. I text Jerry and ask if I can stop by tomorrow and do a couple of songs around six.

He texts back one word. OKAY!

When I get in the house, Mom's in the kitchen, making dinner. "Your grandmother tells me all is mended with you and Emily."

I nod. "Yeah, it's all good."

"Good. I like Emily; I like who you are when you're with her."

I sit and talk with her—random stuff about her day, what is she cooking, then I ask if she's still working until five tomorrow.

"Yes," she says. "Why?"

"I have to run an errand. Would you mind picking me up from downtown? I'll be at a hotel called the Ambassador."

"The Ambassador, where all the stars sleep? What are you doing there?"

"Something for Grandma and me. You'll get me at six?"

She glances up from the pot of stew that she's stirring. "Sure."

"I'll tell Grandma. Thanks." I dash from the chair before she starts asking any hard questions. I knock on my grandmother's door, then go inside when I hear her voice. "I'm doing something big tomorrow. I want you to be there."

She sets down her knitting. "We'll all be there."

"No, it's you and Mom. For now." I go to my room, take Georgia from his case, and hold him tight. After tonight, I'll either have him forever or I won't have him at all.

———————◇———————

Mom and Grandma step through the revolving door, their gazes searching for me in the expansive lobby.

"Hi, thanks." I lean in, give them both a kiss.

Mom glances down and sees the trumpet case in my hand, and her smile vanishes. "What's going on?"

"I want you to come with me for a couple of minutes—"

"Nira, no." Anger and hurt chase their way across her face. "You know what your father said about the playing, what we both said. I can't believe you've disobeyed us! And dragging your grandmother into this!"

"No one drags me anywhere." Grandma turns away to cough. "I'm my own person."

"Mom, I—"

"No, no, no!" She steps close. "This is what you've been doing, isn't it? All those times when you said you were going out for coffee? I thought you had a boyfriend. I didn't like it, but I was a teenager once, I remember. So, I let it go. But this, Nira, this. After everything we talked about—this is your life; this is your future!"

"That's exactly it. It is my life and my future. Mom, please—"

"I'm done. Get in the car." She turns and walks away.

"This is my BBQ!" I call after her.

Her steps falter, and I chase her. "This is my BBQ. Maybe it's not the kind Dad wants; maybe it's not the quality or the price he thinks, but—"

She turns to face me.

"—your BBQ was good enough, wasn't it? Even though—"

"It's not the same. You can't compare your future with some stupid thing that cooks chicken."

"Yes, I can, because you did. Because both of them are about making choices and deciding your own future."

"Nira, don't be silly—"

"You wanted it, you wanted it, and you took it, even though you knew Dad would be upset."

"But—"

"The chicken was very good," Grandma says. "Delicious and juicy."

"Her life isn't chicken," Mom says wearily.

"Just sit for ten minutes," I plead. "If you want to leave after that, you can. I'll finish my set, and I'll tell Jerry I won't do the job."

She blinks. "Someone wants to pay you for this?"

I nod. "Sit, Mom. Please?"

She hesitates, but Grandma doesn't. "Where are you playing? My feet are tired."

Mom gives her a sideways glare. "Really? Your feet are tired from walking for thirty seconds? This, from a woman who walks for hours around the neighborhood?"

"It's strange, isn't it?" Grandma takes my hand. "It must be the difference in the ground."

I lead her to the restaurant and breathe out the tightness in my chest when I hear the sound of Mom's heels following us. We step inside, and I help Grandma out of her neon pink coat.

"Is this new?" I ask as I fold it over my arm.

"Brand-new. Bought it just for tonight."

"Why? We're inside?"

"Look how dark this place is. You can't see a foot in front of you. This—" She jabs the coat. "You can find me anywhere."

"Old woman, aliens on Pluto can find you. This is toxic neon."

"But it looks good on me, doesn't it?"

I kiss her cheek, then flash Mom a smile as she comes through the door. She doesn't smile back.

The restaurant is full, six o'clock is prime time for the dinner rush. Jerry's at the front, waiting. He shakes hands with Mom and Grandma, gushes over my playing. After he seats them and insists on paying for their dinner, he takes me to the stage.

"Mom doesn't seem thrilled to be here. I put them in the back. You won't see her."

"Thanks."

"Has she ever heard you play? Really play?"

I shake my head. "I have ten minutes. If she's not impressed, I can't take the job."

"If this doesn't sway her, then it's because she's deaf." He smiles and leaves me to my work with a parting, "Good luck."

The plug-ins are built-in, and it only takes me a couple of minutes to set up. Then it's showtime. The first song set is a no-brainer. A combination of "Georgia on My Mind," "Fly Me to the Moon," and "What'll I Do?"

I slip into some Adele and Joss Stone because who doesn't love them, then toss in some Al Green for good measure. As I blow the last note, Jerry walks by.

"Your ten minutes are up, and both your mother and grandmother are crying. Keep playing."

And I do.

"Your father will need convincing," Mom says as she turns the car into our neighborhood.

"It's three against one," says Grandma. "What is he going to do?"

"Throw a tantrum, like always." Mom's worried; I see it in her eyes, but there's pride, too, when she looks at me. "You were really good, honey. Really good. Those people at the restaurant, they stopped eating just to hear you play. They were whispering about you, taking video. You really moved them."

"Thanks."

"But I don't know what your father will—" She stops midsentence. Uncle Raj's Tesla is in the driveway.

"This can't be good." Grandma unbuckles from the passenger seat and leads us into the house.

I text Farah, then follow my grandmother in.

CHAPTER TWENTY

INTEGRITY IS GELATINOUS GOO

I drop my stuff at the closet door and trail Mom and Grandma into the kitchen. Uncle Raj and Dad are sitting at the table.

"Your daughter has something to tell you," Dad says.

Mom and I exchange an uncomfortable glance.

"I don't know what you're talking about," I say.

"Tell her; tell your mother where you were tonight." He pauses, deliberately, and adds, "At six tonight."

"I know where she was, Raul," says Mom.

"She told you she was at the hotel." He turns his focus to her.

Mom nods.

"But did she tell you what she was doing there?" He rises. "Did she tell you she was playing that blasted trumpet? The one we expressly forbade her from playing?"

My gaze falls to Uncle Raj, to the smug smile on his face. "You were there."

"Client meeting."

I want to ask which of them was the client, but that would cross a line. I can't stand him, and I'm furious that he hijacked the event just to get back at me for knowing his stupid, dirty secret. But if someone is going to rip off my dad's blinders and show him what a jerk his brother is, it'll have to be Uncle Raj.

He spreads his hands wide. "We're family, Nira. I'm responsible for helping raise you. I know your father and mother told you to stop playing, and I know you defied them." The smile grows. "What kind of brother, what kind of uncle, would I be if I kept quiet?"

"This isn't about my defiance," I say. "This is about your deception, and that I know all about it."

His smile flickers. "You've been caught, don't make up wild tales to swing the attention from yourself."

"I can't believe you defied me, that you disobeyed me." Dad's an angry bull about to charge. "I've been so good—so has your mom. We let you have the trumpet, try out for that stupid band, go to Florida—"

"Florida? That was never for me! That was all about you, and forcing me to live the life you want me to live!"

"Do you hear the way she talks to you?" Raj is standing, speaking in Dad's ears. "Back-chatting you, in front of everyone. No decency, no respect."

"You're grounded," Dad says.

"That's not enough," says Raj. "You should take the trumpet."

"That's mine. You can't have it." I search for Grandma. She's on the sidelines, watching, and she looks like a ref waiting to call foul but letting the players have the field.

"Her trumpet, listen to that." Uncle Raj laughs. "Everything you have is thanks to your parents, Nira."

"He's right," says Dad. "I'm taking the trumpet."

"Raul." Mom holds up a warning hand.

"Get it," says Dad. "Bring it to me."

I shake my head.

"Raul."

"Get it!"

"Raul!"

Dad's head snaps in Mom's direction.

"I know what Nira was doing," she says. "She asked me if she could, and I said yes. Your mother and I were there with her."

The smile slips from Uncle Raj's face.

Dad stands frozen. "You knew? You knew?" The questions come out as a whisper.

Mom nods.

Uncle Raj is smiling, again.

"And you didn't talk to me about this? You told her to lie to me?" Dad's humiliation is complete. His daughter has been lying to him, his wife is part of it, and so is his mother—and now his brother knows.

I'm so tired of this stupidity. "No one told anyone to lie. I asked Mom to come. If she thought it was worthwhile, then we were going to talk to you—"

"If she thought it was worthwhile—" Dad sneers. "She and I discussed it; we decided your marks are more important. And now, the two of you are deciding how you're to be raised."

"It's not like that—" I hold up my hand.

Uncle Raj strokes the lapels of his blazer. "My god, Raul, what is going on in your house."

"Let's talk about this later," says Mom. "When we're alone."

"Oh, now you want family time. He knows, Safiya. He knows you've told your daughter to lie to her father."

Uncle Raj is watching the scene, smiling at the chaos he's created.

Mom and Dad are arguing, and I go to my uncle. "I would never have told anyone. Why would you do this?"

He ignores me and steps away. "Raul, I don't know what's going on in your house, but I don't want my family around it. Farah won't be sleeping over anymore, and she's not to spend any time with Nira any longer."

So that's it. He's threatened because Farah likes us better, worried that she'll eventually spill his secret to the family.

"Nira won't be around anyone, anymore," says Dad. "No more sleeping over, no more Emily, no more anything but school. I let your mother and grandmother steer me away from what's right for you—"

"This isn't about what's right for me. This is about you and this idiotic rivalry with your brother."

"Don't get fresh with me!"

"It's not fresh! It's truth, and you know it." I sweep my hand around the kitchen. "We all know it. Always fighting about who has the bigger thing, the better thing. Whose daughter has the higher marks. If you want to fight, fine, but leave Farah and me out of it—"

Dad whirls on Mom. "Are you happy now? You see what you've done?"

"I didn't do anything—"

"Leave her out of it, too."

Dad dances backward. "Leave her, leave you. Who do you think you are to talk to me like that?"

"I'm the kid pulling down As, and who wants a little freedom to be who she wants to be."

"You think the Ivy League schools are okay with just As? Everyone has As at that school. You have to be better, and blowing on a piece of tin isn't going to get you an admission."

"Yeah?" I can't hide the disdain in my voice. "And when I get into that Ivy League, how am I supposed to pay for it?"

The blood drains from Dad's face. "Scholarships, and don't you ever speak to me in that tone, ever again."

"I'm going to get the scholarships, and I'm going to get into the best schools, but it won't be for math or science or medicine. It will be for music."

"Don't be stupid!"

"I'm not. This is what I want."

"Trumpet? When you can save lives or make a difference—"

"Music saves lives; art makes a difference," I say.

He scowls and waves me down.

"I want this, Dad. You think it'll be any easier to get into those Ivy League schools or get funding if I go into science? Everything's a competition; everything's hard. At least I'll be doing something I love."

"The world will always need doctors—"

"The world will always need music," I say.

"No," he says. "No. You put it down."

"No, I won't. I want this, and I'm going to do this."

"Not if I take your trumpet."

"You can." I shrug even though the idea of losing Georgia shatters my heart and makes me want to howl. "But I'll buy a new one."

"Not if I make you quit your job."

"I'll get another one."

"I forbid it."

"You can't stop me," I tell him. "One way or another, I'm doing this."

"And you'll fail!"

"So? At least I'll have tried."

"Nira." He's disgusted. "This is your life, not some stupid kids' movie."

"That's it, exactly. It's my life."

"You want this so bad you're willing to lie to your father to do it." Trust Uncle Raj to be the snake in the den.

"I want it," I say, hoping it will be the last time I have to speak the words.

"I forbid it," he replies.

I shake my head. "It won't matter. I'll find a way."

"Even if it hurts me?"

I force myself not to cry and nod.

"Even if it's caused this problem between your mother and me?" He gestures to where Mom stands. "This thing is more important than your family."

"It's my face in the mirror, Dad, and I have to do what's right for me."

"Raul," Mom speaks, but he raises his hand.

"Do what you want, Nira. I don't care anymore. End up in the gutter; it doesn't matter what I think."

"Dad, that's not true!"

But he shakes his head and walks away from me.

————————◇————————

My confrontation with Dad fractures the house. He stops talking to me, to Mom, and to Grandma. The next few days are spent in the frost of his icy silence. He won't look at me. When dinner is made, he takes his plate and eats in front of the TV.

Mom signs the hotel contract on my behalf, and she lets me keep my job with Reynolds.

"I'm sorry," I tell her when she hands me the paper. "I'm sorry it happened this way."

She nods but doesn't say anything because she's not speaking to me, either. My only consolation is Grandma. I escape the tension in the house by going on walks with her. Which is a deception, too.

Most of the time, we meet Farah at the corner and go out. It's the only way the two of them get to see each other. Uncle Raj is in full lockdown, and even Grandma's not allowed at his house anymore.

"I don't know why you didn't step in, Grandma." Farah takes a right, and we head to the Ambassador. My job gives me a giant discount on the restaurant, so we're going for dessert and hot chocolate.

"Why would I have done that?"

"Because Nira needed help," she says.

"Nira?" Grandma twists in the front seat, turning to face me. "What did you want that night?"

"Permission to play at the restaurant."

She sucks her teeth. "Really? That's it?"

"Freedom to be a trumpet player."

"Did you get it?" she asks.

"Yes."

Grandma turns back to Farah. "What did she need me for?"

"You could have smoothed it out, made it easier—"

"Sometimes there's no easy way," says Grandma. "Sometimes, you just pay the price."

"Farah has a point," I say. "You could have told them to behave."

Grandma arches her eyebrow. "Your father told you to behave. How did that work out for him?"

———◇———

A few weeks later, I'm exhausted. Not from the added hours of work, or the extra credit I'm doing at school. I'm weary from my dad. He still won't talk to me, barely acknowledges Mom. Grandma can make him talk, but then again, who can stand against that woman?

I'm on the bus, nodding off, hoping for a hot cup of tea when I get home, eager for the rare night of doing nothing. The rhythm of the vehicle rocks me into relaxation, and I'm almost asleep when it slows and wakes me. I lean left to look through the front windshield. Traffic's backed up.

"Great," mutters the burly man in front of me. He raises his voice and shouts down the length of the bus, "How long you think we got?"

"It just happened," calls back the driver. "Half hour, at least."

The man grumbles, and I get up. I move to the front and ask the driver to let me off. "I'm only a couple of blocks from home. I can walk."

He nods and opens the door, and I step through. I speed home, the wind cutting at my skin. The police have the area around the accident cordoned off. I nod at the officer as she waves me to the detour. One of the ambulance men moves, giving me a view of the road, the pieces of metal, and the splash of blood. A flash of color mixed in with the debris catches my eye.

Pink.

Neon pink.

I spin, dropping my bags, screaming and pushing the officer out of the way as I race to my grandmother.

CHAPTER TWENTY-ONE

RESOLUTION IS
AN UNFINISHED CANVAS

We form a circle around the bed, Dad, Mom, me, Uncle Raj, Aunty Gul, and Farah. A grim-faced man in a white coat lists off Grandma's injuries. "I'm sorry," he finishes, "but with her age and the extent of the injuries, coupled with the brain inactivity—"

"There must be something you can do," says Dad. "Something that can save her."

"Mr. Ghani, with her injuries—"

"Yes, yes." Dad waves him down. "Don't repeat yourself."

The doctor's gaze arcs the room, taking us all in, and then addresses my dad and uncle. "Perhaps if you come outside with me."

Uncle Raj and Dad follow him out the door.

"This can't be real." Farah clutches my hand, her fingers as icy as mine. "She has to come back. She has to be fine."

"The driver's fine," says Aunty Gul. "Distracted by his phone. Bloody fool was texting when he plowed into her. She was in a crosswalk with flashing lights." Her gaze is on Grandma, but Aunty Gul's not seeing her. "Amazing, isn't it? He walks away without a scratch. That man. He destroys everything, and he's the one who's fine."

"Tell me it'll be okay." Farah's grip tightens. "Tell me it will work out."

I shake my head, trying to stop the tears. The machines are doing everything for Grandma.

Farah cries harder and presses her face into my neck. I hug her tight and will Grandma to rise from the bed.

The door opens a minute later. Dad comes in, Uncle Raj trailing him.

"There's nothing they can do," Dad says, his voice flat.

Farah sobs.

I want to cry, too, but I'm holding back. I don't know why. I don't know what being strong will accomplish for anyone. Maybe it's for me. I need to keep my head uncluttered by sorrow, so I can pay attention, take everything in.

"They said she was a goner from the moment the car hit her," says Uncle Raj. "She's been unresponsive since."

I don't contradict him, but what he's saying isn't accurate. There was a moment, a second, when she opened her eyes and saw me, and smiled. And I thought everything would be okay, that she would rally and come back. But maybe her smile meant something else. Maybe I was so caught up in the horror and shock of her blood on the road, I didn't get the message she was sending. Which is another reason to keep steady. If she sends another message, I want to get it right this time.

Dad clears his throat. "We have a lot to discuss."

All eyes are on him.

"The doctor wants to know if we'll donate her organs—"

"No!" Uncle Raj slices the air with his hand. "Absolutely not!"

"We need to talk about this," Dad says.

"And I say no."

"As her family—" Dad gestures to us.

"We are her family, Raul, you and me. Not them."

I squeeze Farah's hand. "Grandma has a living will. She didn't want any lifesaving measures, and she wanted to donate her organs."

"No one's talking to you, Nira," says my uncle.

"Yeah," I say. "I realize no one is talking to me, but that's not the point."

The skin on his face tightens.

I turn to Dad and find him watching me. It's the first time in weeks that he's made eye contact, and I want to cry and scream and wail that this is what it took for him to remember he has a daughter.

"She had a living will?" he asks.

"And an estate will, too."

Uncle Raj snorts. "How convenient. Nira's the one who has the information. Nira's the one who—"

"She told me," I say.

"Oh." His eyes go wide with mockery. "Even more convenient—"

"Shut up, Raja Ghani," Aunty Gul speaks quietly. "Shut up."

He jerks back, closes his mouth, and looks at the floor.

"I have copies of them, too," I tell Dad. "They're at home in a folder."

Dad's looking at me like he's never seen me before in his life. "She gave you the papers?"

I nod.

"She didn't even give them to me," he says. "I didn't know she had sorted through everything."

I shrug.

"And you're sure this is what she would have wanted?"

I take my phone out and call up the photo app. "I have digital copies. She was—I always worried about her slipping when we went out." I have no idea how I'm keeping calm, but I cling to the quiet inside of me. "I have the list of her medications, too, not that it matters." I hand the phone to Dad.

He's still staring at me like I'm a new life-form. Dad takes it and reads. "Mom was clear in this. No lifesaving measures, everything donated." He hands the phone to his brother.

"If you ask me—" he starts.

"No one is asking you anything," Farah says.

He shoves the phone at me and stalks out of the room.

"I'll get him later." Dad takes a painful breath. "It's time to say good-bye. Gul, you start. We'll give you privacy." He ushers the rest of us out the door.

After her, it's Mom, then Dad. They both come out crying.

"Farah, you go ahead," he says.

"Come with me." She holds out her hand to me.

Dad stops us at the door and puts his hand on my shoulder. "No time limit. Stay as long as you need."

I nod. After I lead Farah to the head of the bed, I retreat to the background and take a seat in the darkened room. She climbs over the railing, gently shifting and moving until Grandma's arm is around her shoulders, and it looks like the two of them are napping. Farah turns into our grandmother and sobs.

I give her privacy and space until I realize her tears will never stop. She's unspooling in front of me. I go to her and put my hand on her shoulder. She shudders under my touch and presses herself closer to Grandma.

"I want to go with her. If she has to go, I want to go with her."

"Far—"

"But I can't. I never will. She's going to a place I'll never be."

"What are you talking about?"

"She's good, Nira, good in a way I'm not—I hang out with people I can't stand because they make me feel good about myself. I lie to my parents. I smoke—I'm not a good person."

"Don't say that; it's not true."

"It is true!" She can't take her eyes off Grandma. "Even now, my tears are for myself. I'm selfish. Just like my father."

"Definitely don't say that." I pry her away. "Come on, come out of there before you pull apart her tubes." I help her off the bed, then push two chairs together so we can sit.

"I'm not crying for her; I'm crying for myself."

"So am I," I tell her. "So is everyone on the other side of the room."

"You lost a person, your grandmother, but I've lost my everything." She reaches for Grandma. "She was the only one who loved me, and now she's gone. I'm alone. Who will love me now?"

"I love you. Mom and Dad love you. Your mom loves you—as best she knows how."

"But no one loved me like Grandma."

"That's because no one loved like her." I put my arm around her shoulders. "I love you, and I'll never love you like she did, but you'll never love me like she did. But we love each other, and she loved us, and that has to count for something, right?"

"That's a lot of love."

"It has to be. We're her granddaughters, and she was everything that was good and pure in this world."

She holds me, tight and hard. "Don't leave me, Nira, please don't ever leave me."

"I won't."

She hugs me harder. "Promise you won't."

"Unnecessary—I think you've just melded our bodies together."

She laughs, then claps her hand over her mouth. "You shouldn't make me laugh."

"You think Grandma would care if you smiled?"

Farah looks over. "I keep waiting for her to sit up and demand a cup of tea."

"Me too."

She stands slowly. "Your turn now."

"You can stay if you like."

Farah shakes her head. "I needed you for this, but you don't need me."

I walk with her to the door, and when I open it, I see Uncle Raj on the other side. "Go ahead," I tell him. "I'll see her after you."

He's in there for almost an hour, and when he comes out, he's pale and shaking. He looks fragile and young. Uncle Raj stumbles down the hallway. Dad goes after him, but Aunty Gul puts her hand on his arm and stops him. Then she follows her husband.

Then it's my turn. I'm cracked and broken and trying to pretend I'm okay, but now that I'm alone with her, I can't hold it in. I take her hand, trying to tattoo the feel of her skin into my memory, trying to will her back with my love.

But there's nothing I can do, and my love isn't enough to create a miracle. I whisper how much she means to me, laugh over stupid memories, chastise her because I have a bunch of chocolate in my bag and now who will I give it to? I cry and tell her how much I'm going to miss her.

———◇———

A half hour later, we're back to standing in a circle around her bed.

"Will the doctor do it?" Mom fights to keep her composure. "Pull the plug?"

Dad nods.

No one moves to call the doctor, and the room is nothing but the beeps and hissing of the machines.

"She can't go out like this," says Farah. "Not like this." She turns to me. "The last thing she should hear in this world is your music, Nira."

Dad makes a sound, and I brace myself for the onslaught. Rather than a lecture or a dismissal, he says, "She's right. I'll go get it."

"You should stay here," I say. "I'll go."

Dad shakes his head. "You were her granddaughter," he says, like that answers everything.

"I left my bag by the door," I say. "Will you bring it?"

He nods and leaves with my mom.

Aunty Gul says, "Maybe we should get some food for everyone," then she leaves, too.

Uncle Raj scurries after her, then stops at the door. "She was a good mom, the best." He's talking to the handle. "I was lucky. Sometimes you don't know the value—" He sobs and stumbles out the door.

For a long moment, Farah watches the spot he's vacated. Then she turns from it and hooks her arm through mine, and we sink to the chairs.

"In the Tibetan Book of the Dead, they say it takes forty-nine days for the soul to cross over. During that time, relatives are supposed to read from the book to help the loved one find Bardo," says Farah. "Do you think it's appropriation if we do something like that for Grandma?"

"I don't know," I say, "but when has she ever needed anyone to give her directions?"

Farah smiles. "I bet she's already there, making everyone curry."

"Dressed in that parrot shirt—"

"And that neon coat!"

Our laughter splinters into pain. We'll never see any of it again. She and I stay quiet until Dad and Mom come back. They must have texted Farah's parents, because they're right behind mine.

"I told the doctor," says Dad, fighting to get out every word.

"He'll be in soon. In the meantime—" He holds out Georgia for me.

And somewhere deep in my pain is the feeling of rightness. Georgia should be here. He should be the one to carry her to the other side, to heaven or Bardo, or whatever place is celebrating her arrival. I dig in my bag for what I need, then turn to the trumpet case.

I take out Georgia. The whole time Dad was gone, I was scared, terrified that when the moment came, the grief would prevent me from playing. My sorrow is still here, thick and heavy, but this act of love for my grandmother gives me strength. Having Georgia in my hands fills me with peace.

I go to Grandma, hold her hand for the last time, and curl her fingers over a piece of chocolate. Then I go to the foot of the bed, take a breath, and blow. "Over the Rainbow" melds with "What'll I Do?," and it comes together in the song—in my final wish for her—"Fly Me to the Moon." The notes soar and cascade, and I send her my love and thoughts with every breath. Fly to the moon, dance among the stars, I love you, and I love you, and I love you. The last note of the song is what she hears as the doctors disengage the machines.

I let Georgia fall to my side. My grandmother is among the planets and stars now. She is a golden comet, a galaxy of one. I'm left on this earth, on a world that's darker and sadder for her passing, and I don't know what to do without her beside me.

CHAPTER TWENTY-TWO

LOVE IS THE SWEETEST TEA

I t feels wrong to leave her bedside, but when Farah says, "She'd hate us sitting here, staring at her, and crying," I realize she's right.

"She'd smack us all for moping," I say.

Dad nods. "Let's go."

We file out of the room. Farah and I are sandwiched with our mothers on one end and our fathers on the other. As I step out, I see Noah, Mac, and Emily standing by the chairs. I must have texted them—or maybe it was Farah. I can't remember, but I'm not surprised grief has stolen my memory. But, I promise myself, it will be the last memory of my grandmother that it takes. The rest of them I'll hold until the day I die.

"I'm so sorry." Emily starts crying. "She was always so sweet to me whenever I came over." Turning to Mac, she says, "You would have loved her. She would have loved you—and stuffed you with tea and food."

Mac smiles. "I met her. That's exactly what she did. Fed me. I tried to tell her I wasn't hungry, but it didn't matter."

Noah doesn't say anything. He just steps forward and opens his arms. His action is all the conversation I need. I go to him and sink into the warmth of his solid presence. Someone hugs me from behind—Farah, maybe. It doesn't matter, because soon I feel the crush of the other bodies. Even Dad and Uncle Raj are part of it— I can tell by their cologne. We're a giant pile of arms and legs and love.

It hurts so bad, the loss of my grandmother, but weirdly, there's a feeling of comfort threading its way through the pain. It's because of my friends and family. Check that, there are no friends here. Just family.

We're a constellation of hurt and tears, a universe of heartbreak and memories. Shining lights and black holes, comets and shooting stars. Even though Grandma isn't here in person, I feel like she can sense us, and if we quiet our grief, we'll sense her back.

I want to stay buried in the love that surrounds me, to cover myself with the collective strength, and stay immobile until my broken heart mends.

But I hear Mom say, "We should go. We're blocking the hallway." Then we're pulling apart, formed individuals once more, though invisible tendrils connect us still.

"Is it okay for us to come over?" Emily asks. "I know we're not family, but I have these memories of her—"

"Shush," says Mom. "Of course you're family."

"Can we bring you some food?" asks Noah.

Mom shakes her head. "There are leftovers. We can heat something up."

"We'll bring food," says Noah. "You shouldn't have to do anything tonight." Mom opens her mouth to argue, but Noah says, "I remember what it was like when my mom died. Making coffee felt like a big deal."

Her mouth closes. She nods as she takes his hand and squeezes it.

"I have my car," he says to me and Farah. "Do you want to come with us, or . . . ?"

I look at my parents, but before I have a chance to speak, Dad says, "Go with them. I have to talk to Raj."

My dad's easy words signal a change between us. For a second—a split second—I'm left immobile as my world shifts. Then Dad smiles and the ground settles underneath my feet.

We leave the hospital and step into the quiet night. I slide into the passenger seat of Noah's car, while the girls take the back. There's no conversation along the ride; no one suggests turning on the radio. It's just the five of us, silent. Noah holds my hand, and I'm sure in the back seat, Emily and Mac are holding Farah's. Their loving touch and the quiet is all the music that we need.

————◇————

Noah drops Farah and me at the house, then the rest of them go for takeout. Farah and I are a two-headed organism that shuffles to the kitchen. Mom and Aunty Gul are already there, rummaging through the fridge, looking for the mithai Grandma had made.

I head to Grandma's room to get her estate and will.

"Nira." Dad stops me.

"Yes?"

He doesn't say anything; he just pulls me in his arms and hugs me tight. I hug him back. "You did good by her. You always did right by her."

"Thanks." I pull away. "I should get the stuff from her room."

He takes my hand. "I see it now."

"See what?"

He lets go of me. "You're exactly like her." He smiles, starts crying, and turns away.

Memory takes me into her room because my vision is a blurred mess. After I step inside, I don't do anything but lean against the closed door. I keep my eyes shut and feel the echoes of her presence. Grief takes me to her bed, where I trace the faint indentation from her head on the pillow.

I take her pajamas out from underneath the pillow, press them to my face, and inhale the scent of her. My sorrow is overwhelming, but I don't cry. I can't—any liquid on her clothing will erase the smell of her from the fabric. The bed catches me as I collapse. Farah's words sound in my mind—I, too, want to go with my grandmother, to be in any place she exists. The only person who ever saw me—*really* saw me—is gone from this world, and I don't know how to stay upright as everything spins out of control.

"Nira." Dad's voice sounds from the other side of the door. "Are you okay in there?"

"I'm fine." I clear my throat and force myself to sound stronger. "Just finding her papers."

I return Grandma's clothing to their spot under the pillow, then I move and sink in front of her dresser. She'd told me she kept them under the bottom drawer. I pull it out, disengage it from the rest of the bureau, and find an envelope. Time has turned its white surface to gray.

I open the folder and slide the contents on the floor. Inside are a list with her bank accounts, documentation of her stocks and bonds, deeds to her home in Guyana, a copy of her living will, and her last will and testament. There's also an envelope with my name.

I take it in my hand and trace the precise script of her writing. The edges are worn soft by time. I open it. There's another envelope, plus a paper with my name on it. I unfold the letter and start reading.

Nira,

If you're reading this, I'm dead or you're snooping.
I hope it's the latter. There's so much of life I still
have left to live. If I have passed, I hope I died in
the satin sheets of the bed of my much-younger
lover. Maybe a good-looking actor, one with muscles
and dark hair. I'd like to think if he proved too
much for my heart, I also proved too much for his.
What a way to go! What headlines—Hundred-year-
old lady was too sexy for her thirty-year-old lover.

God, trust my grandmother to make me laugh and cry, at the
same time.

I wonder how I will die. I pray it will be years
from now—

I glance at the letter's date. Two weeks ago.

Please, Lord, it wasn't a senseless death.

The letter crumples in my hand.

I'm not going to give you advice on how to live your
life. If I have been worthy of your love, then I will
have lived my life as an example.

I put down the letter because I'm crying so hard, I can't see the paper and am afraid I'll make the ink run. I catch my breath and keep reading.

I have so many hopes and dreams for you. I hope you have all the good things life has to offer, but I hope you have your share of tragedy, too. It is only when our hearts are broken that we see how strong we really are, that we see how much love surrounds us as people reach out.

But Nira, I hope you find strength and comfort in yourself. There are times in this world when you will have to set off on your own, when doing the right thing will mean doing it by yourself. Never fear these moments, never fret the lonely road. It will take you to beautiful vistas and lands of possibilities, if only you trust it. And if you let it, the moment will remind you of how strong you are.

"Nira?" Dad taps on the door.

"She left me a letter." I can barely get the words out. "I'll be there soon."

Now I must turn to the true reason behind the letter. My death. I already know my sons and daughters-in-law will be useless. God bless them, but they won't know what to do. You and Farah will have the level heads needed to take the family through these waters.

I keep reading her letter and log the instructions on the kind of funeral she wanted, including the music and program.

I hold the paper close when I read the lines that blaze themselves on my skin and heart.

Go to your dreams, ignore everyone else. You're just like me, and I got all the dreams I dreamed. I got you and Farah (and your parents, but every dream has a weird part, right?). If I could do it, you can do it. You and me, girl, we're cut from the same cloth.

I hold the letter close, finish reading, then turn to the sealed envelope. It's stuffed, and when I open it, another envelope falls out, addressed to Farah. There's also a pile of tea bags and sugar packets. They're labeled, and I sort them. A tea bag and three packets each of sugar for Uncle Raj, Aunty Gul, Mom, Dad, and Farah. I hold the tea bag for me and search the envelopes for the sugar.

Nothing.

I go back to her dresser, looking through the drawers, even pulling them out to check underneath. I sort through the last one, lifting the clothes aside, and find a folded slip of paper with my name. On the other side are the words, *I know what you're looking for. You don't need it. You're strong, Nira. I love you.*

"Nira?" Farah comes in and kneels beside me. "Is everything okay? You've been gone awhile."

"She left me a letter."

"Oh."

"And one for you, too."

Her legs must lose strength, because she leans against the wall. She reaches for the envelope with trembling hands.

"Are you going to read it?" I hand it to her.

She shakes her head. "Not yet." Her fingers stroke the envelope. "Not yet."

I point to the tea bags. "She left instructions."

Farah moves to the pile. Her fingers play against the sugar packets and tea bags. "Where's your stash?"

I hold up the tea bag.

"No sugar?"

I collect everything and stand. "Come on, I'll make you some tea."

"I don't need tea."

"I'll put the kettle on to boil."

"Don't be a ninny. I don't need tea."

"Okay," I say, "a small cup."

"I'm not—okay, fine, a small cup." She starts down the hallway.

There's the sound of the doorbell. "Nira," Mom calls, "the kids are here."

I move, then stop in the doorway. For a moment, it's like Grandma is here. The air in the room changes. It grows warm and bright. I'm sure I can smell her perfume and hear the sound of her laughter.

Farah stops, turns. "Are you coming?"

I follow her, and leave the door open behind me.